PARIS THIBIDEAUX AND THE WORLD OF LOST THINGS

A Boy, A Dream, A Gift for Making Something Out of Nothing

K F Thurber

For My Family and Friends,
Sincere thanks for your love and kindness

*P*aris *Thibideaux believed in a World of Lost Things . . .*

He was convinced of the existence of this World because pieces of it kept turning up in his yard, in the alley, and in the great green basin of Powderhorn Park—odd bits of busted bicycles, broken toys, and rusty appliances. He was new to the city, and to him the alleys of his neighborhood read like a book that he couldn't put down. In the discards of other people's lives he read stories of loss and abandonment, of hurried departures and broken homes, of waste and want, and all he had to do to change their endings was pick them up.

He moved through the neighborhood like a magnet passing through a box of nails. He was only eleven and until about a year ago, he and his mother had lived and worked in the country, following the harvests from season to season. He didn't know that the City is at once the Cradle of Civilization and the Reject Pile of Humanity—a place at odds with itself, full of contradiction, always welcoming new people and yet always falling apart and away from some previous grandeur that is more remembered than real. And yet, people keep coming to the City as they have throughout history, for opportunity and a better life—immigrants, refugees, the poor, the old, the broken, the lost, the artists and dreamers who don't fit in anywhere else—people like Paris Thibideaux and his mother.

CHAPTER ONE

I t was the summer of the traveling trees, and no one at the City Parks Department was surprised that it was happening in that circus-tent of a neighborhood around Powderhorn Park. The first sapling disappeared from the boulevard in front of Randi Leonardo's house, and reappeared a few days later, replanted in the park overlooking the pond. The second tree wound up on a hill that rose above the park's bridle path.

It was no secret that Randi didn't want a tree. That part of the boulevard hadn't had one for decades. After years of begging the City for a tree, and not getting one, the neighbors simply took over the space for their own gatherings and entertainments. They didn't want to give it back now. When the third tree went missing, the Tree Man from the Park Department went door-to-door to investigate. This threw Randi into a tizzy, and that was how Paris Thibideaux got temporary custody of the tree.

"I've got to get it off of my property before Tree Man gets here. The guy has no room in his head for a new idea. Can you hide it in your garage for a few days?" Randi asked. Paris was only a kid, but

Randi trusted his judgment completely. They looked down at the tree hanging over the side of the wheelbarrow like a drunken sailor.

"The root ball probably weighs forty pounds," she added, crossing her arms over her ample chest, "what do you think?"

"I can do it," Paris assured her, "but we better move fast."

Moments later, Paris was zigzagging among the trashcans and tall weeds that lined the alley behind Randi's house, trying to stay out of sight. For a boy who was fairly new to the city, Paris knew well how to do this. In fact, the Tree Man drove his green truck right past him, as he huddled in the weed-filled space between two garages.

By the time the truck pulled up in front of Randi's house, Paris had just reached what he thought was the safety of his own driveway, but he had thought too soon. A police car was turning into the north end of the alley. In a panic, he dove—wheelbarrow and all—into a great clump of lilac bushes that stood at the edge of the driveway. He worked his way in among the jabbing branches that tore at his shirt and scratched him all over. Out of breath and out of options, he crouched and peered through the leaves and twigs. The car slowed and came to a stop right by the garage, sending a shiver through his body.

Meanwhile in front of Randi's house, the Tree Man got out of his truck. His attempt at door-to-door intelligence gathering had been a waste of time. All he had gathered was a procession of curious neighbors who all knew something but weren't talking. Randi stood over the hole where the three trees had come and gone. She wore a billowing purple dress covered with toucans that made her look like a menacing sofa. A small crowd had gathered round her.

"You're stealing public property, Ms. Leonardo," the red-faced, reedy young man said flatly.

"They're in the park," Randi said, "and you know it."

"The last one isn't," he replied, "what is it with you Powderhorn people? The city tries to do something nice, and you treat it like an invasion."

"Imagine that," Randi countered, looking around at her neighbors.

The Tree Man shifted his weight uneasily, "Come on, where's the tree?

"I don't have it," Randi pronounced, and this was true as far as it went. She did not have the tree—now.

Out back and down the alley, the person who did have it was still hiding among lilacs, trying not to sneeze from the perfume tickling his nose. The squad car was so close that he could see the young policewoman's white-blonde braids. Any minute now, he was sure she would pull out a bullhorn and demand his surrender.

Meanwhile, as Paris cowered in the bushes, the Tree Man tried again to reason with Randi, "Look, the city's putting a tree here whether you like it or not." Randi looked beyond him to the street. He followed her eyes to his truck.

"Aw, geez!" he cried, as a boy reached the roof of the cab, whipped off his shirt and waved it in the air. Several more kids climbed into the empty cargo bay, and three girls started decorating the truck's tires with sidewalk chalk.

"Ms. Leonardo, nobody turns down a tree, *nobody*!" the Tree Man exclaimed, "You got not *one*, not *two*, but THREE trees out of our fair city, and where's the gratitude?"

"I can see that this really pains you and I'm sorry," Randi said earnestly as she signaled the children to come away from the truck, and they reluctantly obeyed.

"Powderhorn," the Tree Man muttered, "I don't get it." And he really didn't. The problem for him was that there were so many people who had come here from someplace else. They came from another city or country with their different languages, different foods, and different ways of doing things. And there were all these kids in the neighborhoods and in the parks who were different from the kids he had grown up with. They were black, brown, yellow, red, white, and eight thousand shades in-between. Their English might be mixed up with Spanish or Hmong or Somali. They seemed to understand each other. He thought maybe they had a common dialect, but whatever it was, he didn't get it, and it made him nervous. As he tried to maintain his composure under mounting pressure, a monstrous heap of a car pulled up and shuddered to a halt right next to the Tree Man's truck.

"BAM! Ba-BLAM!" the car backfired explosively, drawing startled screams from the crowd.

"BAM!" reverberated down the alley to where Paris still hid among the bushes. The cop in the squad car revved the engine and took off in the direction of the sound. A thundering *KABOOM!* shook the air, followed by the sound of muffled cheers. Paris dared to relax a little. He knew that backfire. It could only come from one car—an amalgamated heap of metal that was not so much a car as a loose affiliation of Chrysler, Ford, and Cadillac, with some Toro and John Deere tractor thrown in, if you knew where to look. It belonged to the mechanical wizards of the neighborhood, Blossum McIntyre and Pete Chavez. That rattling, clanking mass of ancient auto parts was now the center of all attention in front of Randi's house, and the Tree Man got the feeling, and not for the first time, that its arrival was a planned distraction somehow orchestrated by Randi.

"I suppose this is just a coincidence," he said skeptically. Randi shrugged.

Behind the wheel of the unusual vehicle, Pete gestured wildly and blasted away in Spanish at Blossum, who was already out of the car and slapping the hood until it popped open. He stepped up on the front bumper and straddled the engine just as the squad car pulled up with its lights flashing.

"You need a tow, Mr. McIntyre?" the officer asked Blossum.

"No, ma'am. We'll get it going in a minute," he said.

"Howard," she called over to the Tree Man, "you okay?"

"Peachy," the Tree Man said, saluting the officer and ducking into his truck.

"Well, okay then," the officer said and drove off.

4

From where Paris remained hidden, he could hear people in front of Randi's house chanting, "BlosSUM! BlosSUM!" Carefully, he untangled the sapling from the lilac bush and stepped out into the open.

Not so lucky, the Tree Man was stuck for the duration of the show. Blossum rolled up his sleeves and, with a flourish, he pulled a length of frayed rope from his back pocket and held it up like it was a string of pearls. Reaching deep into the belly of the car, he wrapped the rope around something and gave it a yank. The engine coughed, "suh-HUHHHH!"

"Do it again!" someone cried.

Blossum was a big man with a mass of salt-and-pepper dreadlocks wrapped in a red bandanna. He had worked with metal and fire for so long that he gave off an almost metallic aura of fiery intensity. From him, combustion engines kept no secrets. Pete, on the other hand, was a short, muscular wedge of a man with thinning dark hair that was usually covered by a backwards baseball cap. Quick and impulsive, he was a master of electricity. In Powderhorn, where old pipes and worn out engines always needed attention, Pete and Blossum were forever in demand. They did a cash-only business, but everyone knew that in a pinch, they could be paid in baked goods, hot dish, or a pitcher of iced tea on a hot day.

Blossum waved his long fingers suggestively over the engine, and wound the rope tightly. This time, when he yanked the cord, the car belched black smoke, lurched against the brakes, and threw him backwards on to the asphalt.

"Give it gas, Pete! Give it gas!" Blossum said brushing himself off.

Pete gave it gas, and the engine purred. Blossum slammed down the hood and took a bow. Applause and whistles followed. The men waved regally to the crowd as they drove away.

Randi approached the Tree Man's truck, "Listen, *Howard,*" she said, "Can't you just skip this spot?"

"No can do, Ms. Leonardo," he said, "I'll be making a full report, and we may have to turn it over to the police."

"I see. Well, don't forget it's Randi with an *I*," she said waving.

The Tree Man pulled away, having had enough of Powderhorn for one day. Meanwhile, Paris triumphantly wheeled the tree toward the gate to his own back yard.

CHAPTER TWO

As he reached for the latch to open the gate, he heard a bone-chilling laugh. He didn't have to look to know that it was Billy McNaughton power-pedaling his bike up the alley. Paris tipped over the wheelbarrow. The tree was heavy, and the burlap unraveled as he hauled it into the yard.

"I'm gonna crush you, Zambo!" Billy roared, skidding and colliding with the overturned wheelbarrow.

"Damn!" Billy cursed. He was a pale freckle-faced boy with red hair and piercing green eyes, but there was no light in those eyes—only a fierceness that set him apart from other kids, and made him old before his time. He ran into the yard, but there was no sign of Paris or the tree, except a dirt trail leading up to the side door of the garage. Paris had a way of *vanishing* that really irritated Billy, who had a reputation for catching anything he bothered to chase. He bombarded the door with his fists. He was a big boy, two years older than Paris, though he wasn't much taller. What he lacked in height, however, he made up for in muscle. If he broke through that door, Paris didn't stand a chance. The tree was propped in the farthest corner of the garage, and Paris cowered behind it staring at the door, straining on its hinges.

"You skitterin' little cockroach, Paris!" Billy shouted, "I know you're in there."

Paris was beginning to feel sick. Every blow to the door jangled his already over-stimulated nerves. "I'm going to die here," he thought, seeing himself lying in a pool of blood with Billy standing over him. Then he saw his mother weeping over his dead body. He opened his eyes, but reality wasn't much better. The old garage shuddered and creaked under Billy's powerful assault. Ancient dust fell all round, strangely animating the atmosphere.

"Hey, *Tibby Dough!*" Billy jeered, "Cajun boy! My Dad says Cajuns are...'

"Shut up!" Paris shouted.

"LOO-zee-ana Swamp Rats," Billy laughed, "and your mom's some kind of Spic Mexican!"

"Stop!" Paris cried.

"You're a *Cajun Swamp Rat Taco!*" he goaded, giving the door a ferocious kick.

Paris felt like he was either going to throw up, or he was going to do something nasty in his pants. He grabbed an old kitchen chair and jammed it up under the doorknob, then braced himself against it. The next time Billy kicked the door, it didn't give as much, and he let out a howl of pain.

"Okay, now I'm a dead man," Paris thought.

There was an ominous silence followed by Billy's hissing through the door, "You can hide now, Paris, but one of these days when you're dragging your raggedy ass around the neighborhood, I'll get you."

Paris barely breathed. He heard the sound of gravel being stirred up, and he moved quickly to a crack in the garage wall that gave a narrow view of the alley. There was nothing in front of him. Suddenly WHACK! —gravel hit the wall, and grit flew into his eye. Paris backed away, his eye stinging and watering. Billy laughed triumphantly on the other side of the wall, but his voice grew fainter. Was he pedaling away? Paris knew one way to be sure. Still shaking, he began to climb a ladder that had been nailed to the wall. It led through a hole in the ceiling just big enough for a person to pass through to the upper floor of the rambling old garage. This "loft" extended only over the back half of the garage and was filled with light from two windows on the alley side. Paris ran to the windows. No sign of Billy.

In the middle of the loft, Paris reached for a thick rope and hauled himself up into a weather-beaten dome that sat on top of the garage roof—a cupola. From the outside, the cupola presented an eccentric profile, but from the inside it was as handy as the crow's nest on a pirate ship. Up here, Paris had the advantage. He could look out over the neighborhood in all directions. Billy was gone, and now Paris could see why. Dan Torvilson, his next-door neighbor, had come out to sit on his porch and read the newspaper, as was his daily custom. He wasn't in the best of health these days, but he still had enough of the old Marine drill sergeant about him to scare off a kid like Billy McNaughton.

Paris shimmied down the rope and walked over to his workbench. It was just a warped piece of plywood that he had attached to two old high chairs. As he stood in front of it now, the fog of fear and nausea lifted. On the ground, Billy could make him feel small and angry and afraid, but up here Paris felt strong, smart and resourceful. Here he had work to do.

When he first moved into the city, the sheer volume of stuff that can accumulate in the city's alleys and dumpsters overwhelmed him. Things wound up in the trash that still had useful life in them, and this bothered him until one day, he started doing little repairs and services for his neighbors, matching found objects and reclaimed garbage to things that needed to be fixed or replaced around the neighborhood. He never read a fix-it book; he simply improvised and discovered that he had a flair for the work. Toy truck wheels made a sagging gate move smoothly again for his neighbors, the Torvilsons.

A large plastic bowl he found in a junk pile marked "free stuff," turned out to be the perfect liner for a leaky old birdbath in the Christenson's back yard. His solutions to common problems were well received, but he worked anonymously. He was not interested in being fussed over for being a clever child. Also, it was a good way to pass the long hours that his mother was away at work, driving a delivery truck for the Paradise Bakery. He was never bored and began to feel something he had never felt before: that he belonged here.

Paris was not the kind of boy to spend hours sitting in front of a TV or playing video games. He preferred to be outside exploring the junction of Lost and Found, which he believed mystically, came together in Powderhorn. He could see beyond dirt, dents, and missing parts to the inherent usefulness of things. The mysteries of appliances from hair dryers to can openers, record players to lawn mowers, fell away before his inquisitive mind. All of his good deeds were marked by a pigeon feather as his only signature, and they were always delivered under cover of darkness.

Like a priest he felt called to his work. It was deeply satisfying in ways that he didn't completely understand, but he was sure it had something to do with his father, who had left when Paris was barely six months old. That was a story whose ending he longed to change, but bringing back lost people isn't as easy as bringing back lost things.

CHAPTER THREE

I t was getting to be dinnertime. Paris stepped out into the late afternoon sun. His mother was just coming through the gate with a grocery bag in each arm. For more than a year now, Marina Thibideaux had been working shifts and double shifts, and then coming home to work on the house. The long hours were beginning to take a toll. She had shadows under her eyes, and her shoulders sagged under the weight of the grocery bags. He hurried to meet her. He had a bounce in his step that reminded her of his father, and she smiled even though it was a little disconcerting—like seeing a ghost.

"What's for dinner?" he asked, taking the heaviest bag.

"Grilled cheese," Marina said, and then she noticed his shirt, which had been demolished by the activities of the day, "Honestly, Paris, do you go to war with your clothes every day? We don't have money for this," she added, as they entered the house.

Paris escaped to the bathroom. He ran a warm washcloth over his face and neck and washed his hands. Sometimes, when he looked in the mirror, he tried to find his father by subtracting his mother's features. Before him stood a brown boy, wiry and strong, with dark eyes shaped like almonds, clear and alert, wide-set in a face the color of coffee with cream. His mother's eyes. His hair was black and glossy as a crow's back, straight and thick "like your father's," his mother had said, but her mind had closed long ago on the subject of his father, and she didn't like talking about him. Paris at eleven, however, had a mind of his own, and like the rest him, it was growing and changing and opening up to possibilities. Maybe, living in Powderhorn had something to do with it, a place where so many things came and went back and forth between Lost and Found. Why not people?

As he scrubbed, Billy's words came back to him. *Spic, Zambo, Cajun*—so many ways to make "not white" sound like a curse. He tried sending them down the drain with the grime of the day, but they left a stain on his heart, which was already overburdened with uncertainty when it came to his lineage.

He came into the kitchen while Marina was listening to phone messages. The old answering machine was spattered with paint and held together with duct tape. When she saw Paris, she put a finger to her lips. He did an exaggerated tiptoe over to the refrigerator and grabbed a couple of carrots from the vegetable drawer. A recorded voice was saying, "Uh, hi Marina. Andy here. Why don't you make me dinner this weekend, and I could help you with the house . . ."

"Who's Andy?" Paris asked, as Marina hit the *erase* button.

"Somebody from work," she said, sifting through a stack of mail.

"Why don't you let him help?" Paris asked.

"I don't need his help," she said, as she tore open an envelope.

"Really!" Paris said playfully, grabbing the letter from her hand, "How long is that wall paper gonna sit in those bags behind the door?"

"I don't know," Marina laughed, snatching back the letter, "I kind of like the look of all this spackle."

"Maybe he knows how to do wallpaper," Paris pressed on.

"He's a baker. He probably doesn't know adhesive from a hangnail," Marina said dismissively, "now, let me read this letter from the bank."

"How do you know? Maybe, he's great at it," Paris persisted, crunching his carrot noisily. Marina tossed the letter on the counter and started pulling dishes from the cupboard.

"Honestly, Paris, if you want Andy to come over so badly, *you* can make him dinner."

"Geez!" Paris said, heading for the living room.

"Wash up!" she called after him.

"Already did," Paris said as he swept a tool belt and a drop cloth from the coffee table. With the TV remote in one hand and the carrots in the other, he sat down and started channel surfing. He would have flopped on the couch, but it was covered with tools and do-it-yourself books. Sawhorses, ladders, and gallons of paint cluttered every corner. The Thibideaux house was a work-in-progress.

In the kitchen Marina turned on the radio to the Latino station. The music brought back memories of her childhood, going from labor camp to labor camp, season to season with her parents—too much hard work, too little money, and no real home. Alone in the world now with her son, she accepted that she might always have too much work and not enough money, but she was determined to give Paris a real home. And this house was going to be *it* if she had to work twenty hours a day to make it happen.

Bright yellow cheese slices on white bread. *Tomatoes. Onions.* She liked tomatoes in her grilled cheese, but Paris preferred onions like his dad. A little butter on both sides of the sandwiches, and they were ready to toast. She turned up the heat on the griddle, and absently began to spear sweet pickles with a fork. A half-smile rose to her lips as she arranged pickles on a plate. It was only a half-smile because with Paris's father, it had been only half-happiness, a crazy mix of Cajun *zydeco* and Mexican *salsa*—fun while it lasted, but ultimately inharmonious, except for one beautiful note they had managed to make together: Paris.

"Mom, come here quick!" Paris shouted from the living room, "The parade is on the news!" Marina switched off the radio and joined him. On the screen, a green school bus rolled by. Half of its roof had been cut away and replaced by a towering apparatus that looked like grasshopper legs. Everyone knew it as the "Hoistabus" because it was an old bus that had been "customized" for lifting engine blocks out of cars. Blossum waved from behind the wheel, while Pete puffed on a fat cigar and sat cross-legged on the roof, tossing candy to the spectators.

"It's Dan!" Marina exclaimed when Dan Torvilson appeared as a clown in a yellow fright wig and giant sunglasses.

"I can't wait to be in the parade," Paris said.

Randi Leonardo appeared next to a reporter.

"This year's Powderhorn Parade promises to be the best ever," the reporter enthused, "I'm here with Randi Leonardo, and this is her *twentieth* Powderhorn Parade, right?"

As Randi began to talk about the parade, the video showed footage of last year's parade.

"It's a great mish-mash of cultures and traditions—stilt walkers, drummers, puppets, horns, rattles, and bells – and then there's the Free Speech section for all our activists!" She went on to enumerate: "Anarchists, Socialists, Pacifists, Animal Rights, Human Rights, and The-People-Who-Wear-Nothing-But-Kale," Randi laughed, "which *wilts*, you know, on a hot day."

The reported interrupted, "It sure looks wild and extravagant, but it's actually carefully planned and lovingly built over several months each year. From the ragbag, the basement, and the attic, it emerges: miles of fabric, vats of glue, and truckloads of glitter and feathers."

The video revealed the parade route lined with people waving from rooftops and porches, and blankets spread out on lawns. They camped out on the tree-lined boulevards with beach chairs and coolers full of snacks. There were wagons full of toddlers; young fathers with babies strapped to their chests; and, infants nursing under mothers' shawls.

Marina and Paris were spellbound until the distinct smell of burning toast invaded the living room. Marina ran to the kitchen with Paris at her heels, and flipped the charred sandwiches onto the counter.

"This is what happens when we don't pay attention," Marina said under her breath.

CHAPTER FOUR

She scraped away at the blackened surface of the bread, and without comment Paris poured lemonade into tall glasses of ice. In silence, they returned to the living room with what was left of their dinner. The TV had been taken over by the sharp, hard sell of a cheap real estate commercial.

It's the Absolute FASTEST And Easiest Way To Put Tens of Thousands of Dollars In Your Pocket! Make millions flipping houses! It's market-proof. You win when real estate values go up; and, you STILL win if they go down!"

"Oh, please turn that off!" Marina begged.

"I'm trying!" Paris said, desperately whacking the sluggish remote against the arm of the sofa. Marina seized it. Paris tried to grab it back.

"Wait!"

"No!"

Still, the commercial droned on. *Let the buyer do the work and pay YOU for the privilege!*

Click.

Marina tossed the remote on to the couch. Paris looked puzzled.

"What?" she asked.

"Well," Paris said thoughtfully, "isn't that like your deal with Mr. Ermler? You do all the work on the house, and you still have to pay . . ."

"No!" Marina turned on him coldly, "absolutely not."

She stacked their plates and carried them to the kitchen. The sleazy commercial had started Paris wondering about the "special deal" his mother had worked out for buying their house from their sleazy landlord, and now her reaction was making him wonder even more. She was washing the griddle in an extra noisy, splashy manner.

"Next year for sure," she said scrubbing forcefully, "we should both be in the parade, don't you think?"

The words *next year* hit Paris like a thunderbolt.

"Last year, you said *this* year we'd do it," Paris said, unable to hide his disappointment.

"Did I?" Marina said absently, rinsing and splashing away, "Well, the house comes first. You know that."

"Why do I have to choose? It's not fair," Paris retorted.

After living in trailer parks, labor camps, run-down apartments, and homeless shelters, he was as eager as his mother to have a "home" and to "stop the wandering," as she put it. But other things were rising in importance for Paris, and while Marina had been busy driving for the bakery and working on the house, Paris had been joining in the life of the neighborhood. The parade expressed and embodied that life. He wanted her to be part of it. He tried another tack.

"I have a great idea for a float," he said pointedly.

Marina turned up the flow of water and chattered on, "You know, Paris, that letter I got from the bank says I can get a loan as soon as all the repairs are done."

"Want to hear my idea?" Paris persisted.

She turned off the water, "Did you say something?"

"My idea. For a float," he said.

Marina frowned, "*Next* year, Paris. Right now, we've got to put everything into the house."

"But the parade's important, too," Paris insisted.

"Not if it gets in the way of the house!" Marina said, "We have to be grown up about this. When I get that loan, we will own this house."

"Well, *great!*" Paris said, twisting the lid on the jar of pickles and slamming the jar on the counter.

"It *is* great," Marina snatched the jar and put it in the refrigerator.

"Super," Paris declared, turning away from her and staring out the kitchen window. Someone had dumped an old toilet in the weeds across the alley.

After a moment of silence, Marina spoke more calmly, "Well, I have to go to bed. I'm due at work by five a.m. We can leave the dishes till tomorrow."

"'Night, then," Paris said brusquely.

She came up behind him and hugged his shoulders, "Next year after the house is done, we'll do the parade. I promise."

"I want a glass of milk," he said, pulling away.

"Come up soon," Marina said. Before going upstairs, she turned out the lights like she always did. In the dark, Paris opened the refrigerator. He breathed in the cool air and drew it around him, turning his body in the eerie glow. His shadow danced on the dimly illuminated walls and ceiling. He let go of the refrigerator door, and as it closed with a magnetic click, the dark of the house closed in around him.

CHAPTER FIVE

In the morning Paris awoke to an empty house. Marina had left before the sun came up. He went downstairs and made himself two peanut butter and jelly sandwiches. One he ate for breakfast, and the other he wrapped in waxed paper, and stuffed into his back pocket. Into a big canvas sack, he put more food for the day—an apple, Oreos, and carrots—and slung it over his shoulder. When the food was gone, the bag would be a fine receptacle for whatever dropped from the World of Lost Things. Finally, he filled his water pistol with milk, took a swig from the carton, and dried his hands on his jeans. As soon as the back door squeaked on its hinges, the yowling began.

"Come and get it, you guys! Kapow! Kapow!" he taunted, dancing backwards down the alley in the direction of the Torvilsons, and drawing the herd of cats after him. When he pulled the trigger, the cats twisted and leaped to get a lick of milk. Next door on the Torvilson's porch Zippo, an old tomcat with a white coat stained the color of ashes, dozed indifferently. Dan called Zippo "the General," because he had outlived his enemies and had the battle scars to prove it, including one torn and furless ear that looked like leather. Dan's mother Helen just called the cat "Shoo." Zippo spent his days either basking in pools of sunlight on the porch, or hiding from Helen Torvilson's broom. Dan spent his days similarly, though not so much in fear of the broom.

Dan and his cousin Tommy Browneagle were sitting on the back porch, on an old couch that was supposed to go to the Salvation Army but never quite made it. Before them lay a plush carpet of grass. It looked as though a strip of emerald velvet had been dropped by angels on to a bed of weeds and hard-packed city dirt.

Tommy called out to the alley, "Hey, Paris, where ya been—kinda late for you, ennit?"

Although Dan and Tommy were cousins, there wasn't much of a family resemblance. Tommy looked more like his Native American father than his Scandinavian mother, Dan's aunt Irene Torvilson. The Torvilsons and the Browneagles had grown up together in Northern Minnesota, but it wasn't until Adam Browneagle married Irene that they became family as well as friends. Dan's parents moved to Minneapolis after World War II. Adam and Irene stayed up north, but during the summers, Dan and Tommy went back and forth between the city and Leech Lake. They were more like brothers than cousins, and after high school they joined the Marines and went to fight in Vietnam.

Paris had a hard time picturing Dan and Tommy as young crew-cut Marines. Nowadays, Tommy had long, steel-gray hair that he tied back with a strip of leather. He was a big man, a little broader in the middle than he used to be, but still in pretty good shape. In contrast, Dan had blonde hair that had gone stringy and dull. It stuck out like straw from under his faded golf cap. He started to cough, and Tommy handed him a beer. It was a little early for beer, but these days Dan had no use for clocks. The coughing subsided as Paris let himself in at the gate.

"Do not disturb that feather," Dan said. It was what he said to anyone who came in that way.

"My mother's crazy about the way that thing works now. Whoever put the little wheels on that crooked old gate was pretty ingenious."

With an inward smile, Paris turned his attention to Zippo, running his hand along the cat's bony back.

"Morning, Zippo," he said.

Zippo blinked one heavy eyelid. Paris raised the pistol of milk, and the cat was instantly alert. He caught some of the spray and licked the rest from the porch. When he was done, he squinted into the sun three times and crumpled into a heap. He was asleep before his belly hit the floor.

"Now, that's real sleep right there," Dan said, "I'd like to be the General for half a day so I could sleep like that."

"You *do* sleep like that," Tommy joked.

Paris began to climb the big maple tree that shaded most of the Torvilson yard. When he reached the branch with the homemade birdfeeder shaped like a little wooden house, Tommy handed up a bag of feed. This was a task Paris had taken over from Dan, who couldn't manage it any more. Paris lifted the hinged "roof" of the birdfeeder and poured in the seed. He let go of the empty bag, and it drifted down into Tommy's outstretched hands.

"Dan, the latch is bent," Paris announced, "I can't get it to close."

"Damn squirrels," Dan said.

"Looks like they chewed away some of the wood," Paris explained.

"Maybe, you should take it down," Tommy mocked, "birds are getting fat the way you feed them all summer."

"I like fat birds," Dan said, taking another swig of beer.

"It's okay. I got it to work," Paris announced from his perch in the tree.

Tommy nudged Dan, "Get up, dude. It's your turn to putt."

Dan rose slowly. He had always been a lean and lanky guy, but he had grown very thin lately. He was losing his hair, he seldom shaved, and he had given up caring about most things except the game of golf. This was the sad truth behind all the jokes that passed between the cousins.

It was Tommy's idea to create the "putting green" in his cousin's back yard, and it quickly became Dan's favorite place to be. Also, it was a sacred place (really) blessed by a medicine man from Leech Lake. Paris and his mother had attended the ceremony, along with a few of the neighbors. They had burned tobacco and said prayers, and Tommy's drum group had played. Afterwards, they feasted. Marina loved the Native American soup made with *mahnomen*—the wild rice of Northern Minnesota—but Paris couldn't get enough of the Norwegian *kransakake*—concentric rings of cake stacked on top of each other to form a tall pyramid drizzled with icing and decorated with tiny paper flags of Norway, the U.S., and the American Indian Movement, AIM.

"Oh!" Dan cried suddenly, doubling over.

Tommy put his arm around him, and Dan let him until whatever-it-was had passed.

"I'm okay," Dan said straightening up, "*really*," he added, looking up at Paris, whose fears he wanted to dispel.

"So, Paris, are you going to be in the parade this year?" he said with a wink.

The question took Paris by surprise.

"I don't know," he said doubtfully. According to his mother, he was supposed to forget about the parade. Dan squinted up at him and fished out a cigarette and lighter from his shirt pocket. Paris had seen the lighter many times before. It was what they called a Zippo, old and tarnished, kind of like the cat. It had a map of Vietnam etched on one side and the Marine Corps insignia on the other. Dan lit up and put the lighter away.

"What do you mean, you don't know?" he asked, "You are or you aren't, which is it?"

"My mom's real busy," Paris said.

"You need your mom?" Dan asked.

"No. She needs *me*," Paris said defensively.

Dan exhaled and watched a thin stream of smoke rise and dissipate in the air.

"Oh, I almost forgot!" Paris exclaimed, "we saw you on TV last night. They showed the parade from last year on the news."

"No kidding," Dan said, "I missed it."

"You were the best clown," Paris added earnestly, "Will you do it this year?"

Dan thought a moment and then said, "I've kinda *been there, done that*, ya know? Not lookin' for glory any more—just the bottom of the cup."

"Yo, Dan! You gonna putt or pontificate all day?" Tommy interjected.

Dan took a few practice swings, moved into position over the ball, and then froze. Just when Paris and Tommy were beginning to think he'd gone to sleep, he made his putt. The ball stopped at the lip of the cup.

"Dang, I need a new putter," Dan said.

Tommy laughed, "You need an alarm clock."

"Seriously, this one's not workin' for me," Dan said.

"Seriously," Tommy replied, "you've been kickin' my ass with it pretty regular."

Dan smiled, "Well, that's true," he said, tapping the ball into the cup, "but bending hurts my back. I need a belly putter."

"You and Fuzzy Zoeller, eh?" Tommy said.

"Hey, Fuzzy says if it helps people stay in the game, why not? I'm gonna put an extension on one of my old putters . . ."

"It's time to go to the doctor, Danny," Helen Torvilson interrupted, "you don't want to miss your appointment, do you?"

"I kinda do, Ma," Dan said, rolling his eyes. He dropped another ball and began lining up his next putt.

Helen's Norwegian roots were never far from the surface, especially when she was worked up, as she was now.

23

"Ya, no!" she said definitively, "I'm not playing around. Let's get going."

She was a tall, big-boned woman who wore her long hair pinned in a swirl at the back of her head, exactly the way her mother had worn hers. She favored loose cotton dresses in summer, and the one she was wearing today fluttered temptingly in the vicinity of the sleeping Zippo, who swiped at it like he suddenly remembered he was a cat.

"Shoo!" she cried, and Zippo shooed.

"Relax, Ma, the V.A. can wait," Dan grumbled.

"No, it can't, 'cause those cancer cells don't wait. Come on now," she barked.

"Oh, ya!" Dan mimicked.

"Come on, Dan, stop bein' a baby," Tommy teased.

"You boys make fun all you want, but Danny has to go for treatment."

Dan sucked on the last of his cigarette. He flicked the butt into the coffee can he had nailed to the porch rail. It landed with a satisfying *ping!* From inside the small cloud of smoke that he had created, he said to no one in particular, "If I wasn't so darn good at it, I'd probably quit smoking."

"Daniel Johann Torvilson . . ." Helen steamed.

"Ma," Dan said gently, pointing toward the tree, "say hi to Paris."

"Oh hello, Paris," she said, "I didn't see you up there."

"Hi, Mrs. Torvilson," Paris replied as Dan followed his mother into the house. Tommy sat down heavily on the couch. Immediately, Zippo jumped on to his lap. Tommy rested his hand on the old cat's back. Then, he closed his eyes and let his head fall back on to the cushions. He and Zippo went somewhere far away behind their eyelids.

Paris climbed down from the tree and left. It was easier than standing around wondering why bad things happen to good people.

CHAPTER SIX

Paris spent the rest of the morning and a good part of the afternoon in his garage contemplating and sorting the stock of scrap metal, baling wire, and assorted lumber he had been accumulating with no clear idea of how he was going to use it. Well, that was not exactly true. He knew that it was for a project that was coming together in his mind: "something" (he wasn't sure what) for the Powderhorn Parade. He had been gathering stuff for almost a year, and his mother's being against it now, was not enough to stop him from thinking about it. He sat cross-legged in the middle of the floor and "let the junk talk to him." He had an intuitive process, a chain of feelings like stepping stones that he followed until it led him to start picking and choosing, and eventually designing and building even his smallest projects.

A few nuggets of metal from his workbench clattered to the floor, and Paris realized he wasn't alone. Zippo was a frequent visitor to the workshop and had his own secret ways of getting in whenever he wanted. The old cat circled and sniffed things warily.

The difference between this and Paris's other projects was that this would not be a repair; it would be something built from scratch. All afternoon he organized and sorted his raw materials, and for the first time the scale of the thing he wanted to build began to take shape in his mind. He moved everything he thought he might use to the first floor where he had more space. The light fell from above and made the dust swirling in the air look like bits of crystal. As he stared at the unrelated pieces, a large figure began to rise in his imagination. Zippo woke up and looked at him quizzically. Paris leaned over and whispered in the cat's furless ear. If Zippo thought he was nuts, he didn't let on.

The light had shifted into that late afternoon brightness that reminded Paris that it had been a long time since his last snack, and he was hungry. When he went into the house, he found his mother asleep at the kitchen table with her head resting on her arms. In the center of the table was a pie she had brought home from the Paradise Bakery.

Paris nudged her gently, "Mom, I'm home."

"Oh, hey," she greeted him, blinking the sleep away, "I must have dozed off."

"Maybe, you should go to bed," Paris said, allowing himself to be hugged.

She brushed the hair away from his face, "Help yourself to mac and cheese. It's on the stove."

He went about serving himself.

"Wash your hands," Marina said. He trudged to the sink.

"How's Dan? I brought him a cherry pie from the bakery."

"Nice, but he probably can't eat it," Paris said, "Mrs. Torvilson took him to the doctor today, and he's always sicker after that."

"Poor guy. I'll take it over tomorrow," Marina said.

Paris lifted a carton of orange juice to his lips.

"Get a glass!" Marina insisted.

"*Wash your hands, get a glass!*" Paris mimicked.

"Come over here, I want to show you something," she said, opening a home repair book with many dog-eared and coffee-stained pages. She pointed to a photograph, "This is a beam that runs all the way from the front of the house to the back. Here, where they've opened up an entryway, it's called a header."

Paris sat down and began to read while she talked, "I had to put a brace in the middle of ours because back in the sad history of this little house, somebody stupidly chopped out a big chunk of it for wires or something, and it started to sag like two inches."

"Mom!" Paris gasped, "it says right here 'Concerning your beam, *you should call in an expert* if you observe *cuts or notches*, especially those made along the *bottom of the beam*; or, a *sag* in the middle of the beam of *3/4 of an inch* or more.' It doesn't say 'Moms, feel free to do it yourself!' I mean, shouldn't we hire somebody who knows what they're doing?"

"I know what I'm doing, Paris!" she demurred.

"No, but . . ." Paris began.

"Okay, that's it! Dinner can wait. We'll just do this now."

She pulled him by the arm into the living room.

"First of all," she said as they stared up at the header, "my brace is not strong enough. We need to reinforce it. I need to wedge in this four-by-four, and you're going to help."

Paris noted that for a small woman, his mother had a mean grip and no fear of lumber. When she was focused on a job, she could tune out everything and everybody.

"Now hand me that bar for leverage."

"Mom, what are you trying to prove?" Paris asked testily.

"I'm going to ease the weight off of the brace so we can reinforce it with a four-by-four. I want you to lean hard against this, and on my signal, *push* with all of your might. Understand?"

Paris nodded without enthusiasm. Reluctantly, he got into position.

"On THREE," Marina said, and she counted "One, two, THREE!"

Paris pushed and pushed and pushed some more. The house groaned.

"Harder, Paris, you're slipping!" she cried.

"I can't help it," he wheezed, "Mom, this is nuts!"

Marina's entire being was committed to this impossible task. She grunted and groaned like a beast of burden.

"Mom, stop!" Paris cried in fear and desperation.

"Get out of there!" Marina sputtered.

Paris scrambled out from under, and part of the brace crashed to the floor.

Marina gasped and quickly put it back together, nailing extra pieces of scrap lumber over the cracks.

"We need HELP!" Paris exploded.

"No!" she shouted.

"We need a guy!" he blurted.

"There *is* no guy, Paris!"

"There are lots," Paris countered, "you just hate them all!"

"You don't' know what you're talking about!"

"Yes, I do! If my Dad came back tomorrow . . ."

"Your dad?" Marina fumed, "You don't even know what he looks like!"

Paris's eyes narrowed to angry slits, "And whose fault is that?"

"His!" Marina shouted.

"I wish he took me with him!" Paris shouted back.

"Well, that would have made *my* life a lot easier!" Marina barked.

He took the stairs two at a time, and slammed his bedroom door, leaving Marina to ponder her words. She returned to the kitchen and the dinner that never got eaten. Mechanically, she moved the pot of mac and cheese from the stove to the refrigerator and started to wash the dishes that had been left in the sink from the night before. What kind of mother, she asked herself, demands a man's strength from a boy and then tells him that her life would have been easier without him?

CHAPTER SEVEN

Night fell. Paris switched on the flashlight that he kept by his bed. He curled his fingers in and out of the beam of light, making shadow shapes and figures dance on the walls when there was a soft knock on his door.

"Paris?" Marina called in a voice just above a whisper. She opened the door and slipped inside, coming to stand silently by his bed. He switched off the flashlight and did not look up at her.

"Can I sit?" she asked.

His answer was to move over an inch. She reached to turn on the lamp.

"Don't!" he growled.

She sighed, "I'm sorry I said those things. I didn't . . ."

"I don't care," Paris said, cutting her off, "Where's my father?"

"Paris, you *know* I don't know."

"You never tell me anything about him. Why did you even marry him?"

He turned away from her, "Never mind. I don't want to know."

"If you give me a minute," Marina said, "I'll try."

Paris kept his back to her, but he listened intently for Truth.

"Your Dad was with a rodeo," she began, "I was working on a farm with my family, and we went to see it."

She smiled, remembering, "He was very good-looking and he was good at a lot of things, especially training horses and riders. We both knew right away that we wanted the same thing. We had grown up on the road, always moving. Working since we were kids. We wanted to settle down, make a home. We thought . . ."

Paris turned to face her, "Why'd he go away, then? It doesn't make sense."

Marina looked out the window like the moon could give her the answer.

"You're right. But that's the way it was. He meant to stay, but he just couldn't. It wasn't his fault, exactly."

"Whose fault *was* it then?" Paris insisted.

Her long, dark hair fell around her shoulders and created a shadow over her face. The warmth of her old blanket bathrobe came through the sheet as she sat next to him on the bed. He used to love snuggling up against it when he was little and hurt or sick, but he fought the urge to do that now. He clicked on the flashlight and resumed making shadows on the wall.

Marina looked at his resolute expression and felt weak before it, "Paris, I tried to find him. I really did."

"I don't believe you," he said coldly.

Marina stiffened, "Well, it's true. Ray Thibideaux *wanted* to disappear, and he was good at it."

"What's that supposed to mean?" he sputtered.

Marina was angry now, "He had a powerful need to be alone, and he would just disappear—and I couldn't live like that, not with a baby."

"So you threw him out!" Paris said, accusingly.

"No!"

"Forget it," Paris clicked off the flashlight, and in the dark his words rang out, "I had a father and you lost him."

"No! He lost *us!*" Marina protested, turning on the lamp.

Paris got up on his knees and shouted, "How come there's not ONE single thing of his! I've got nothing. You did that!"

"Yes, I burned it! All of it!" she yelled back.

Until that moment, mother and son had not shared this particular Truth.

"Where?" he asked.

"In the desert—where he left us," she said.

"And then you almost gave me away."

"*Almost.*"

This was the part of the story they had recited to each other since Paris was a toddler.

"Because you didn't know how to take care of me, but then you learned," he prompted.

"Yes, you taught me what I needed to know," she replied.

His tone had softened when they reached the familiar part of the story, but the next time he spoke, his words were sharper than ever.

"People are not like things," he said icily, "you can't just throw them away!"

"I'm sorry," Marina said thickly, "but every time I tell you more about your father, I feel like I'm losing you to a ghost that isn't here, and isn't real. *I'm real. I'm here. Always.* Doesn't that count for something?"

"I want to know his side of the story," Paris said.

"Well, I can't help you there," Marina said, wiping her eyes with the hem of her bathrobe.

Somewhere, there *was* Ray Thibideaux's side of the story. Only Ray could tell it; and he wasn't talking. But history is in the blood, too; and it has a way of surfacing whether we put words to it or not. When Paris was a baby, she could pretend that he was all hers, but clearly Paris was no longer a baby. Soon, he would be a young man, and she wondered, as she never had before, if she would do better with him than she had with his father.

"Good night," Marina whispered, bending to kiss his cheek.

31

As the door closed behind her, Paris slid his hand under his pillow and pulled out a rough-edged fragment of paper. A click of the flashlight revealed his secret treasure: a family photograph that had been torn apart. Paris had found it wedged between the pages of a book while they were packing for the move to Powderhorn. He had kept it to himself, and that small deception separated him forever from the child-world in which he had believed that his mother was always right.

Even though his father's face had been torn away, Paris could see his baby self in the picture, sitting on his father's knee. He could almost feel his father's hands holding him. Maybe, Ray had torn himself out of the picture just before he tore himself out of their lives. Maybe he had worn those very same boots on the day he walked away from his wife and baby. Cowboy boots.

At the end of the hall, Marina opened a door and stepped out onto a small balcony overlooking the yard and the alley beyond. The ledge was just wide enough to stand on, or to shake out dust mops as people did back in 1905 when it was built. It was only the second floor, but there was a significant difference in the air. Having grown up on ladders and in trees picking fruit with her family, she felt at home in high places. It was a starless night. The only light came from Pete and Blossum's place, the blue flashes of a welder's arc. They had opened up the garage, and the cool riffs of a tenor sax drifted out on the night air. The guys liked to listen to classic jazz while they worked. Bathed in the eerie, pulsing glow, a shadowy form was making its way southward. It was Randi's unmistakable figure pushing a wheelbarrow with a small tree in it, headed for the park no doubt.

Paris fell asleep with his hand under the pillow, resting on the picture of his family.

CHAPTER EIGHT

I t was a bright sunny morning with a clear blue sky, and Paris woke up full of purpose. The alley was bathed in a peaceful golden glow, and the lawn mowers had yet to begin their daily assault on the grass. With his skateboard tucked under his arm, and a broken tricycle in hand, he crossed the alley to consult Pete and Blossum on a repair question. Suddenly, the peace was shattered by a terrific blast. A plume of black smoke billowed from their garage. Pete appeared, looking like he'd been shot from a cannon, the frayed stump of a cigar clenched between his teeth. From inside the garage, came Blossom's booming voice, "Cigars, Chavez! You can NOT light up in here!"

Pete's face was splotched with greasy, black soot. He seemed to be sobbing.

"What happened? Are you okay?" Paris asked, trying to help Pete sit on a nearby tree stump. But Pete would not be lead. He was doubled over in laughter, not tears.

"Shhhhh!" Pete tittered, putting a sooty finger his lips, "I got to lay low till Blossum calms down."

"What were you doing?" Paris began again, looking closely for signs of a head wound.

Delicately, Pete plucked pieces of the cigar from his mouth and fanned the air before his face, "Oh, nothin'," he said, and to Paris's surprise, he turned his full attention to the heap of things Paris had dropped, "Whatcha got there—something for the parade?"

"No," Paris said, "I'm trying to fix this tricycle, and I rigged up something, but it didn't work. So I thought maybe you guys . . ."

"For sure!" Pete exclaimed, "Come on. We'll see what we can do. But let's take the scenic route and give Blossum a minute to cool off."

Paris was happy to walk with him around the yard, which was littered with old vehicles and defunct appliances. He had always felt a kind of kinship with Pete and Blossum because, like him, they saw value where others saw only junk. They were geniuses at cannibalizing old wrecks in order to keep some newer wrecks moving, and they were adamant that their "inventory" of fallen artifacts was not a *junk*yard. It was *The Garden of Scrap*. A framed sign, mounted on a stake in the ground said so. Among the scattered pieces of furniture, washers, lawn mowers, and other household discards, there were other "exhibits" with their own artfully labeled signs: Broom Forest, Bucketville, and the kids' favorite, The Tower of Toilet Tanks. But cars and the remains of cars were the primary features of The Garden of Scrap. Some had been there so long and sunk so low that they looked like they were growing out of the earth. Creepers and other vines had taken over their interiors, and time and weather were claiming the rest.

Finally, after a suitable interval, they arrived at the garage door.

"Yo, Blossum!" Pete called.

"Yo, Pete!" Blossum appeared at the door, apparently ready to forgive and forget, "You okay?"

Pete glanced reassuringly at Paris, and said, "Oh, yeah. Paris is here to consult with us, though."

Blossum was wearing a leather apron in spite of the heat. His skin glistened with sweat, but he was feeling hospitable and invited Paris to "Come on in."

Paris found that the clutter *inside* matched the clutter outside, but there was one corner that was hidden behind a curtain that hung from ceiling to floor. Presumably, it was the secret province of this year's parade project. At this time of year, Pete and Blossum always became super competitive and mysterious. They treated everyone as a potential spy. They belonged to a neighborhood fix-it man tradition that depended on word-of-mouth for business. The parade had become their calling card. Their eccentric and elaborate projects won prizes and brought them business. As much as they liked Paris, they were a little wary of his youthful energy and talent, and couldn't help seeing him as competition.

Generally, the garage had a lot in common with Paris's garage except that Paris had accumulated only a year's-worth of stuff, and he was way more organized than Pete and Blossum. Their walls were lined with machines and gadgets like statues in an ancient temple, and the "temple" air smelled of gasoline and battery acid. Music, however, softened the impact on the senses. The outsized reels of an ancient tape recorder were playing jazz that the guys had recorded long ago. It connected them to times and places that Paris had never heard of, but he liked the music because it was warm and smoky and inviting. The recordings were like the remains of a distant and strange world inhabited by beings with names like Dizzy and Monk and Holiday.

Pete bounced forward on the balls of his feet, moving Paris along like a push broom, "Paris needs some advice on something. Might be his FLOAT!"

"No," Paris declared emphatically, "it's not for the parade. It's just Lydia's tricycle. Her Grandma Vang threw it out, and I'm trying to fix it."

He wished he had never told anyone how much he loved the parade and wanted to be in it.

"Let's have a look!" Blossum said quickly. Paris held up the tricycle for both men to examine. It was obvious that he had tried to replace a rear wheel with a line of roller blade wheels, but had failed to make a strong enough attachment.

"I would put a metal bar on the bottom—something solid to give it strength where you attach the wheels," Blossum said.

"I could do it with a weld or two," Pete offered.

"Really? That would be great," Paris responded, "Can I stay and watch?"

"Sure, but don't crowd me," Pete said, pulling his mask down over his face.

Paris was the only kid they allowed inside the garage. They admired him because he had great instincts for spotting serviceable scrap metal and they enjoyed his enthusiasm for their work, but they never let him forget that Blossum's forge was a serious pit of fire, and welding is not a youth sport. Grasping a round piece of metal with heavy black tongs, Blossum examined it closely. His deliberate movements contrasted sharply with Pete's perpetual motion. As Blossum pumped the bellows with his free hand, he talked himself through the steps. Paris loved to watch Blossum work, but at that moment he was drawn to the way the rhythms of jazz were working through Pete and into his welding. He got a little too close, and Pete's muffled voice boomed out from under the mask, "Hey, get back!"

Blossum gently guided Paris away, "Come over here . . . man with the fire stick's a little touchy about his space."

He led Paris to a cart that was piled high with car batteries, gauges, and coils upon coils of copper wire.

"This is what we call the Juice Cart," Blossum chuckled, "Watch."

Every time Pete zapped a weld the needles on the gauges bounced, and the cart shuddered noisily. Blossum touched a wire to a contact, and a colossal whip of pure electricity leaped and crackled.

"Wow!" Paris exclaimed, "Can you guys teach me?"

Blossum shook his head, "Your mother wouldn't like that at all."

"Please!" Paris begged.

"Maybe next year," Blossum added.

Pete stopped welding and removed his mask. He took a long look at Paris and said, "When it's time, it's time."

Blossum stiffened, "No, sir! I don't think so, Pete! Marina will *kill* us!"

Defiantly, Pete picked up an extra pair of insulated gloves from the bench and offered them to Paris, who took them eagerly.

Blossum shook his head, but didn't intervene as Pete slid the welder's mask over the boy's head and stood behind him.

Blossum threw up his hands "I suppose there's nothing I can . . ."

"Nope," said Pete, "just turn on the juice.

"I don't like this one bit," Blossum mumbled as he got the Juice Cart going again.

Arm-to-arm, and glove-to-glove, Pete guided Paris while letting him get the feel of welding. The music had changed, and Pete passed on the new rhythm to Paris. DZZZT! It's one thing to see the flashes of light and the shower of sparks, but now Paris could feel it. DZZZT-DZZZZZT! Right down to his toes! What a great feeling—all the fun of being a boy, and all the power of being a man at the same time. Blossum kept looking over his shoulder, expecting to see Marina.

"This is how I learned when I was only a little older than you, Paris," Pete said, "My Daddy taught me."

"You have a steady hand for a kid," Blossum said approvingly.

Pete raised his mask and inspected the bar that was now attached to the tricycle's wheel mount and said, "Some day, I'll show you how to do the big stuff."

Blossum moaned and made the sign of the cross.

"It looks darn good," Pete announced, "we can drill two holes through it so you can bolt the roller blade wheels to it."

"Thanks!" Paris gushed, "I'll pick it up later, okay?"

"Sure," Pete said, as they started for the door, "where you headed?"

"The park," Paris said, picking up his skateboard.

"Listen, while you're out and about, I could really use anything that looks like that," Pete said, pointing to a taillight, "and I mean *anything*.

I'm getting desperate. Seems like an epidemic of fools backing into taillights."

"Okay. I'll see what I can do. What's this?" Paris asked, picking up a metal rod about a foot long that had been lying by the door.

"Motorcycle kick stand," Pete said, "you want it?"

Paris turned it over, considering the possibilities, "Could you straighten out the curve for me?"

"Well," Pete said, "you come through with *my* stuff, sure."

"Deal," Paris said, as they walked toward the alley.

"Come on, Paris, is this something for the Parade? You can trust me, man," Pete pleaded.

"Gotta go, see ya!" Paris said impishly, and took off.

Pete sat down on one of the old toilets at the base of his "tower," lit a cigar, and contemplated the passage of time. Only yesterday it seemed he was a boy learning from his father the skills he had just imparted to Paris. He had no children of his own, and he had never missed having them until now. In Paris, for the first time, he saw a boy growing into the powers of a young man, walking away more confidently than he had arrived that morning; and, Pete was proud and a little astonished that he had had something to do with it.

CHAPTER NINE

At the end of the alley, Paris dropped his skateboard and hopped on. It was a perfectly sunny day, and the sidewalk stretched out before him like a long gray ribbon leading into Powderhorn Park. It was a city park that defied expectations. You could almost forget that you were only about ten minutes from skyscrapers downtown. The lake formed the bottom of a great bowl, and in the center of the bowl was the island, densely covered with trees. Today, clouds floated on the water's surface, and in the distance horses grazed in the large fenced-in pasture known as The Meadow. It was a remnant of another time—a time when horses outnumbered automobiles.

Usually, when Paris went to the park, he didn't join the other boys playing basketball or swimming in the pool. Often, he made for the trees. Up in the shady canopy of a tree, the wind riffled invitingly through their leaves like a dealer shuffling cards. The leaves tickled his arms and legs and brushed against his cheeks. He would find a broad branch from which to watch the hot summer world move in slow motion below. That's when he would retrieve the extra peanut butter sandwich from his back pocket. Though slightly squashed and molded to the contours of his backside, the jelly-soaked bread melted in his mouth like cotton candy. The peanut butter gave it the perfect mix of salt and sweet. As he licked the purple ooze from the crusts, horses and riders moved easily with the early morning breezes through the dappled light that fell on the bridle path below. Paris liked to straddle the branch and pretend he was a rider who wanted no company but his horse. There was one particular horse—she was a dark chestnut with white markings on her legs and a star-shaped splash of white on her face. He imagined that with a friend like her, he could take a vacation from the human world of words.

One day he went up to the Meadow. The horses moved away from the fence as he approached, but the chestnut came back. When he looked into her dark eyes, she looked back with equal interest. She seemed to be as curious about him as he was about her. She lowered her head invitingly, and he ran his hand down the length of her face from forehead to muzzle. He stroked her long neck, reaching up under her mane and following the line of her long neck muscles down to her shoulders. It was a privilege that he hadn't expected. He felt *chosen*.

Today, his heart beat a little faster with anticipation as he left the street edge of the park and took a diagonal path toward the interior. He angled the skateboard downhill on a stretch of pavement that merged with the lower path around the lake. This took him past the back of the park building and toward the barn. All kinds of earth-movers and dump trucks were at work preparing the site for the new horse show arena. For the most part, the barn was a typical old and sturdy design, but it had some unique features. On the roof, it had seven ancient lightning rods poking up at the sky, and four metal ventilators that looked like teapots without spouts. On the ground, the constant beeping of back-up alarms agitated the birds, particularly the herons that nested on the island. They swooped and hovered but would not light while the noisy machines were at work.

The workers were always shooing kids away from there, but not Paris. All he had to do was think and move in a certain way, very calm and very focused on his destination, and people seemed to stop seeing him, or simply accepted him as part of the scenery. Like a jump roper preparing to jump into Double Dutch, he would align himself with the pace of things going on around him and merge with the flow. He stashed his skateboard in some bushes and passed through the work area unnoticed.

Inside the barn was showing its age. It had scrapes and nicks in the doors and walls, but it was clean and organized, and it was home to more than horses. Sparrows and other small creatures hunted, played, or dozed up in the rafters. Paris slipped through an open stall door as easily as air and dove into the fresh hay that billowed up from the floor. He was ready now for the game that he and the horse played when no one was looking. Almost immediately his nose began to itch, but he barely breathed as a young woman led in the horse and prepared to start grooming. The big animal, her coat warmed by hours in the sun, carried heat and the scent of grass into the small cubicle. Paris swallowed hard to keep from sneezing.

"Okay, darlin'," the groom said at last, "a little hug for you and I'll see you tomorrow."

As soon as she left, the horse lowered her head to where Paris was hiding, and when her grassy, oatsy breath hit him in the face, Paris sneezed explosively. The horse was taken aback momentarily, but she almost knocked Paris over trying to get the treat that she knew was in his bag.

"Geez!" Paris laughed good-naturedly, offering her half of a carrot.

"I bet you're going to be in the parade again this year," he murmured, "I wish I was."

He spoke softly, telling her his troubles as he could tell no one else. This was the main reason he had come today, to bury his sadness with a friend he could trust. But his friend suddenly tossed her big head and knocked him to his knees. Stunned, he tried to get up, but she stepped forcefully in front of him and pinned him against the wall. Someone was coming. The stable manager had caught him once before. Luckily, she let him off with a warning, but she had promised to call his mother if it happened again. With that disagreeable thought in mind, Paris dove into the hay again, barely breathing. Like a wily conspirator, the horse turned her attention to slurping noisily at the water bucket. The footsteps passed. Paris stood up and brushed himself off.

"Thanks," he whispered, giving her a big hug, "see you later."

The door slid closed with a thud. Paris wanted to break into a run, but he forced himself to walk deliberately toward the front doors of the barn. A moment later, he was outside, picking up his skateboard. The park had shifted into its afternoon gear. It was filling up with basketball players and team practices. Reaching the upper path, Paris found himself looking down on a strange and wondrous sight. Apparently stalled on the lower path, at the bottom of a great hill, was the same green City of Lakes truck that had been in front of Randi's house, with the same Tree Man peering under the hood. And in the truck bed, glowing rhythmically was what Pete would have called a "boodle" of flashing red lights. They blinked on and off, winking invitingly at Paris.

The Tree Man jiggled something under the hood, slammed it shut, and got into the truck. It lurched forward and began to climb the steep hill. With the jolting forward momentum, a few of the lights slid off the back of the truck. The engine stalled again, and when the Tree Man restarted it, the truck lurched forward and continued up the hill. Paris followed along on the path above, moving stealthily from one tree or bush to another, counting flashers as they cascaded from the steeply angled flatbed. Apparently oblivious, the Tree Man drove the truck over the top of the hill, leaving the flashers scattered on the path. Like a hawk, Paris swooped down and swept them into his bag.

CHAPTER TEN

"These are *elegante*," Pete enthused over the flashers, "but just in case Blossum asks—you came by these honestly, right?"

"I just scooped them up from the path," Paris said, which was true in all the essentials.

"*Ah-mazing!*" Pete crooned.

"So, did you straighten that kickstand for me?" Paris asked.

"Come and see," Pete said, leading the way, "Blossum! Paris is coming to pick up his kickstand, you decent?" Pete laughed.

Blossum stood by the workbench, where the kickstand lay like a silver scepter on display on top of a piece of red flannel. It had been straightened and polished, too.

"Pete shined it up for you, in case it's going on prominent display," Blossum added.

"It's not for a float!" Paris protested, placing it in his canvas bag, "but thanks."

"Where to now?" Pete inquired.

"To see Dan," Paris said over his shoulder.

"Wait!" Blossum said, glancing at Pete, "Might not be the best time to visit,"

"Yeah, he's probably sleeping after his treatment," Pete added gently.

Paris stopped at the door and said, "I forgot."

"Good man, Dan," Blossum said.

"The best," Pete agreed.

"See you later," Paris said and went out the door, glad to end that conversation.

At the gate to his own yard, he paused. The big locust tree that shaded his neighbor's driveway beckoned to him like a friend, and Paris accepted the invitation to climb up and out of Time for a while.

Every time he climbed this tree, he remembered Max Christenson saying, "A good climbing tree needs a boy or two workin' it, so any time you want to take on the job now that my boys are all grown, feel free." To a boy like Paris with no extended family, Max embodied the kindness of a grandfather. Paris thought now about the neighborhood boys who used to sit where he was sitting, who were now grown men. Dan was one of them, along with Tommy and the Christenson boys. But nothing ever stays the same. Most of the time, he had no quarrel with that. You grow, you change. Usually, it's a good thing. Simple addition. You get bigger, stronger, smarter. Life would be easy if that's all there was to it, but sooner or later there's subtraction. You scrape your knee. You lose something you love. You lose people. There's no word for how bad that feels. Still Paris had Hope. He hoped that one day he might see his father striding toward him. He still had hope for Dan in spite of the devilish cancer treatments. And he had hope for his mother, that the house would turn out all right and she wouldn't always have to work so hard. One thing about the World of Lost Things, there was always Hope.

CHAPTER ELEVEN

A dusty old pick-up truck rumbled into the alley. The driver craned out of the cab window, scanning the house numbers posted on each garage. As usual, there were children playing in the alley. Mrs. Vang appeared and started shooing the kids off to their respective homes faster than a mail sorter. Of all the Hmong people in the neighborhood, Mrs. Vang was the most venerable figure. She had appointed herself the alley Safety Patrol, and although her English was dodgy, she made herself understood to the driver by standing in front of the truck and waving her arms. When all of the kids were out of the way, she stepped out of the path and waved him on.

The truck looked like a scarred old warhorse. The load in the cargo bay was piled high and covered with a shiny silver tarp. Bright red straps and a network of bungee cords held it in place. Suddenly, it stopped and backed right into Max's driveway. The driver got out, and Paris could see even from his place in the tree, that his appearance was very much in keeping with the look of his vehicle. He wasn't a young man, although he was tall and muscular, and he moved haltingly, as though his back hurt. He didn't look up, so Paris couldn't see much of his face beyond his stubbly beard. He looked scruffy, and his dark skin had the leathery look of someone who spends a lot of time in the sun. His hair was wavy and thick and curled loosely over his collar. Like his beard, it was heavily streaked with gray, which accentuated his dark eyes and eyebrows. Even from above, the set of his jaw and his cheekbones looked like chiseled stone. The stranger bent over and placed his hands on his knees, stretching his back. Max and Two-Ton came out of the house.

"Hello, there!" Max said warmly, leaning on his cane and extending his free hand. The man straightened up slowly and clasped Max's hand. Two-Ton, a massive dog with a mottled coat of black-and-brown and a half-white face, moaned suspiciously, but the stranger calmly extended his hand for the dog to sniff, and that seemed to be enough to satisfy Two-Ton.

"Mr. Kovac, welcome!" Max said warmly, "The apartment is all ready . . ."

"Ko-vaCH," the man enunciated.

"Oh! Ko-vaCH . . . " Max repeated, "sorry."

The man nodded, "No problem, you call me Janos."

"YAH-nos!" Max repeated, reaching to help the stranger release the straps that held down the tarp.

"No, thank you," Janos said firmly, "I can do it myself."

He was almost fierce in his movements, although from time to time he had to stop and stretch. He rolled up each strap and tossed it through the open cab window. As he did so, Paris noticed that his left hand had a curious indentation on the outside beneath his little finger, like a chunk of flesh was missing, and the pinky and ring finger on that hand seemed frozen stiff from some old injury. For Paris, this only served to heighten the sense of mystery surrounding his new neighbor.

Determined to make the new tenant feel welcome, Max chattered pleasantly about the charms of the furnished upstairs apartment that he and his wife had been renting off-and-on for twenty years.

"And if you need anything, we live right downstairs," he concluded.

"I know," the man said.

Everyone knew. Max's apartment was like the guest room of the neighborhood. It was a kind of holding place for people who were "in-between" jobs or stages of life. They could stay there for a while without long leases to sign or big deposits to pay. Max never had to advertise. People just wound up there, the way most things wind up in Powderhorn, which is to say, each in his or her own way.

The best thing about the apartment, in Paris's opinion, was the back porch. Exterior stairs led up to it from the driveway, and it had a broad wooden railing painted white that contrasted nicely with the dark green of the house itself. A mature maple tree grew in the yard below and shaded the porch like a natural umbrella. Sitting up there, you were almost sitting in the tree.

At last, Janos whisked off the tarp. He let it billow like a parachute, but before it touched the ground, he gathered it in an instant, pulling it arm over arm into a small bundle, and tossed it into the cab. Paris leaned so far forward to get a good look that he nearly fell out of the tree, but it was Max who exclaimed, "Wow! That's some old machinery you've got there! I haven't seen a radial arm saw like that since the Fifties. It looks like new!"

"No, is very old. Where do I get in?" Janos asked.

Max pointed to the stairs, "You go right up those stairs, and your entrance is off the rear porch."

Just then Two-Ton threw himself at the stranger's feet and pawed the air like a puppy.

"Two-Ton, heel!" Max commanded, embarrassed for the big dog's loss of dignity.

Unmoved, Janos asked, "And key?"

"C'mon, Two-Ton, quit that now," Max pleaded.

"Key?" Janos repeated, turning an imaginary key in the air.

"Oh, the KEY, you betcha!" Max said, "On the kitchen table. Everything's open."

"Thank you," Janos said, starting for the stairs.

"Any questions, you just ask me or my wife Solveigh anytime," Max said, still eyeing the dog skeptically, "C'mon, you," he muttered.

Reluctantly, Two-Ton got up and ambled after his master. Before going into the house, though, the dog looked back over his shoulder. Only he had noticed Paris in the tree.

CHAPTER TWELVE

Peering down through the tree branches, Paris recognized many of the tools in Janos's truck—a radial saw, a drill press, a jigsaw. His mother often said, "If I had the right tools, I could finish this house in half the time." It looked like some of them might be moving in next door! Although the tools looked like they had been meticulously cared-for, just about everything else Janos Kovac owned looked old and abused. His duffels had patches on their patches, and most of his "luggage" was plain grocery or garbage bags. There were two boxes of books, but Paris couldn't read any of the titles. They were not in English.

From the passenger side of the cab, Janos pulled out a box that was a little bigger than a shoebox. It was held together by reams of yellowed tape and little else. Janos handled it with the care one reserves for something precious, but the back of the old box popped open like a milkweed and released a flurry of photographs. Janos stood over the mess and said bad things about God. Stiffly, he went down on one knee to gather his things, muttering in a language Paris didn't need to understand to know that the words were curses. At last, the stranger stood up, hugging the splayed box and loose photographs protectively to his chest. As he paused to catch his breath, Paris noticed a patch of light pinkish skin, stretched taught at the base of the man's neck like a piece of wrinkled satin. Only part of it was visible where the shirt had been pulled aside, but Paris was sure that it was a scar, a big one that might extend all the way out to his shoulder. He wondered if the man was an old soldier like Dan or the victim of some horrible accident.

Janos climbed the stairs and went into the house. This time, he closed the back door suggesting that he was not coming back right away. Paris came down from the tree and approached the truck. He knew that what he was about to do was nothing less than trespassing on another person's privacy, but his curiosity drove him on. He stepped up on to the rear bumper and then over the tailgate and into the cargo bay, where he hunkered down among the tools. They were old, nicked and stained, but the metal had the clean smell of oil, and the wooden grips and bases—having lost their varnish long ago— were worn smooth and gray. These were the loved and respected tools of a craftsman. He wondered what Janos would think of Pete and Blossum, and the motto that hung over their garage: "Grease, Grime—Genius." He knew they would think this truck was a little too tidy.

With no idea what he would say or do if Janos caught him, Paris flipped the latch on a plain, varnished wooden box and found that it held an assortment of chisels, small handsaws, and instruments he had never seen before. They were elegant, kept as lovingly as any jewels. Reverently, he closed the lid and replaced the box in its original position. The grace of that moment was shattered by the coarseness of the next, which carried the sounds of someone breaking glass and grinding it underfoot. Once again, Paris knew that Billy McNaughton was asserting his dominion over the alley. Smashing glass was one of his favorite pastimes, and from the sound of it, he had a lot of light bulbs to kill. He was still a couple of houses away, but Paris did not want to risk being found by Billy or Janos. He had to move quickly. Flattening his body against the truck, he flowed like liquid over the side and underneath, curling up next to a rear tire.

Everything was a potential target or entertainment for Billy. He lived in a mean world without a mother, and with a father who had quit trying to be civilized long ago. Nobody brought up the subject of Billy's mother unless they were looking for a bloody nose. Ever since she left, he and his father Harold had lived alone. Harold spent most of his time drinking, ignoring the neighbors, and dodging housing inspectors. Billy had been on his own in the streets and alleys since he was old enough to reach a doorknob. Their yard was littered with empty beer cans, and the smell of garbage hung in the air. No wonder Billy was seldom there.

A light bulb hit the side of Janos's truck and shattered, evidently aimed at a squirrel that skittered under the truck past Paris. Billy swaggered into view (his feet actually), coming right up to the truck and circling it. He opened the door of the cab and stepped on to the running board. Paris could hear him rummaging through Janos's stuff.

"Hey! You! Get out of there!" a booming voice cried out from the balcony.

Billy jumped down from the truck and bolted into the alley. Janos charged down the stairs like a human tornado, but Billy was already out of reach, bounding through familiar yards and leaping fences. Meanwhile, Paris was stuck. Janos slammed the cab door shut and began violently kicking the front tire. He pounded on the hood of the truck. Paris flinched with every blow. Although he was all too familiar with Billy's bullying rage, he had never been exposed to the rage of a grown man. His mother's anger was entirely different. She tended to fume and fuss rather than to shout and pound things. She was always afraid of breaking things she couldn't afford to replace.

As Janos calmed down and the physical assault subsided, Paris opened his eyes. Directly in front of him, lying near the front tire on the passenger side was a photograph. Paris had a deep regard for photographs, perhaps because he only owned one; and, to him, it was an open window into a world where he and his father and mother were still together. Naturally, he wondered what world was captured in the stranger's photograph.

"What's going on there?" Max called out from his kitchen window.

"Nothing," Janos said, "Some kid stole my camera."

"Want me to call the cops?" Max asked.

"No cops," Janos said, then added, "you know kids around here?"

"Some," Max said, "did you get a good look at him?"

"Red hair? Fast runner," Janos said.

"Oh," Max said, "that would be Billy McNaughton."

"You know him, then. He is trouble, eh?"

"He's trouble, all right," Max said earnestly, "but his father's hell, if you know what I mean."

Janos stared at the ground like he was reading something down there.

"I wait," he said thoughtfully.

"Expensive camera?"

"Old camera," Janos said.

He retrieved the last duffle bag and a toolbox from the cab, and locked it. A few minutes ago, he had come down the stairs like a tornado, but he made the return trip up to the apartment much more slowly and deliberately. At last he reached the top, and went in, closing the door on the world below.

Paris heard the faint tinkling of bells coming from Mrs. Vang's garden across the alley. She was probably watching from behind a screen of morning glories, or maybe kneeling and listening behind a curtain of climber beans. She had probably seen everything, but Mrs. Vang knew when to let things be.

Paris crawled on his belly to the front of the truck, grabbed the photograph, and rolled out from under the truck. Standing out in the open, he noticed that he was covered in dust and dirt. No time to look at the picture now. He slipped it into his rear pocket and made a run for his back door, where his mother was waiting for him. She skipped all greetings, grabbed him by the shoulders and marched him toward the stairs.

"Take a bath," she commanded.

"Max's new tenant just moved in," he said excitedly.

"Get a move on."

"He's got a truck and a ton of . . ."

"Now!" she insisted.

In his room he studied the photograph. It was more like his own precious photograph than he could have imagined. Both were old and cracked and torn, but whereas someone had purposely torn his father out of the picture, Janos had purposely tried to keep his picture together with bits of tape. Within the frame of tattered white edges, a young and proud man stood among other young people smiling and embracing each other. Janos looked happy. Paris understood instantly: *He belongs there.* Even though the colors were faded, the scene looked festive and alive. The woman next to Janos was very pretty. Her dark curls fell to her shoulders. Janos held her close. Paris wondered where she was now.

CHAPTER THIRTEEN

After his shower, Paris pulled on pants and a T-shirt from the pile of clean laundry on his dresser. As soon as he opened the door and stepped into the hallway, something made him stop. He sat down on the top step to listen. His mother was talking with some-one downstairs, and it didn't take long to figure out that it was Felix Ermler, their landlord. He had a habit of stopping in unannounced from time to time, and wheedling Marina into giving him a tour of her progress on the house. Once he even brought "an associate" with him to show off his "model tenant" and the work she was doing on the house.

"It's rude," Paris had said, "why do you put up with it?"

"Because," Marina said, "he's offered us something we can't get anywhere else: the chance to buy a house of our own." What she didn't say, but Paris was beginning to grasp, was that this was part of the price that a low-income single mother had to pay to own a home.

At the moment, Ermler was apologizing with an insincerity that even Paris could hear from upstairs, "Sorry to barge in again, Marina. I did say *knock-knock*."

"What's wrong? You got my payment, didn't you?" Marina asked.

"Oh, sure," he said dismissively, "I've been meaning to stop by, but I'm so busy. Can we just take a quick look around?"

"We're about to have dinner," Marina demurred, "Can it wait till my day off?"

"We have to talk now," Ermler smiled as he came forward and placed his briefcase on the table, "I think you're out of your depth with this house, Marina, and I hate to see you put any more money or sweat into it."

"Is this a joke? I'm about to get a loan!" Marina exclaimed.

Paris could tell that Ermler wasn't joking, and he didn't care about the loan. He had come to talk, not listen.

Ermler cleared his throat, "I have to protect my investment, even though I offered you this house out of the goodness of my heart . . ."

"Hold on! I thought *I* was the investor here," Marina interjected.

"I have another buyer, Marina," Ermler said, each word a little bullet striking its mark, "and he made me a better offer."

"Another buyer?" Marina echoed in disbelief, "A better offer? We had a deal!"

"Yes, but you don't seem to understand it," Ermler said coolly, "it's business."

"You said I could pay you off early if I could get a loan from the bank, and that's what I'm doing," she countered, her voice rising to match the level of fear growing in her gut.

Paris had come downstairs and was standing in the kitchen doorway where Ermler could see him.

"I feel terrible about it," Ermler said, giving a nod to Paris, "but you and the boy are going to have to vacate in thirty days."

"Thirty days!" Marina repeated, following Ermler's gaze and seeing Paris.

"Unless you come up with the money by then," Ermler added, "that's what the contract allows, and I always abide by the contract."

"You can't do this," Marina said forcefully, with what seemed like her last ounce of confidence.

"I have to give you thirty days, so there it is. It's business," Ermler said, and looking to Paris, he added, "I wish I didn't have to do this . . ."

"You don't *have* to do this," Marina cut him off, "I have a letter from the bank about the loan, and the contract gives me six more months."

"No," Ermler said, his voice rising, "the contract says I can cancel any time, as long as I give you thirty days."

Marina felt paralyzed.

He snapped open the clasps of his briefcase and the sound of metal clicking on metal drew all eyes to the paper Ermler withdrew from within.

"Be practical. I brought you a picture of another property that would be great for you," he smiled, reining in his temper, "See? I wasn't going to leave you homeless!"

Marina and Paris stared at the hateful picture.

"It's a shack," Marina said flatly.

"It's down by the railroad yard. The neighborhood's not as nice, but I'd be willing to, you know, take whatever money you've already saved as a down payment. You could fix it up as an investment and sell it for a profit. It's a win-win."

"Just go," Marina said, her voice shaking in spite of her efforts to hide it.

"Think about it, and give me a call," he said, as he let himself out.

Mother and son stood like statues until they heard his car start up and drive away. Finally, Paris spoke.

"Mom, what are we going to do?"

Marina walked over to the drawer where she kept the silverware and yanked on it so hard that it fell off of its rollers and sent the contents clanging to the floor in a heap of mixed utensils.

"Shit!" she said.

"Mom!"

"You heard him," she snapped, "he's throwing us out."

"What about the loan and all your work?" Paris demanded.

Marina shrugged.

"Well, I'm not moving!" Paris declared, "Do you hear me? I won't!"
She glared at him like her soul was on fire.

"Won't?" she said, "Really? When you pay the bills around here,
Paris, you can tell me what you *will* and *won't*! In the meantime . . ."

"No!" Paris shouted, pushing past her.

"Where are you going?"

"Out!" he shouted, "I can't breathe in here."

He could not have known the power of those words to open old
wounds. Marina collapsed into a chair. It wasn't so much the slam of
the back door as those words that shook her to the bone. *I can't breathe
in here.* Those were Ray's words coming out of her son's mouth.

CHAPTER FOURTEEN

We all wake up sooner or later to the fact that our parents are not the towers of strength that they seemed to be when we were little. They can't give us everything we want or need. They can't protect us from everything that might harm us. First, we can't believe it; then we get angry. Eventually, we forgive them for being human; and, if we have children of our own, we hope that they too will forgive.

Paris's rage had propelled him out of the house and deposited him several blocks away before he slowed to a fast walk. He was waking up to his mother's limitations, but he was nowhere near ready to forgive Marina, first for buying into Ermler's phony deal; and second, for giving up. Until today, he never would have believed that his mother could be bullied, but Felix Ermler had done it. She had folded right when Paris had expected the most from her, and she seemed to be angrier with him than at Ermler.

He aimed for the park out of habit, to lift his spirits and breathe easy. The trees in the park brushed the sky and the air always seemed fresher and cleaner for it, but not today. With not even a ripple on the still waters of the pond the atmosphere was stale and uninviting. From where he stood on the upper rim of the park, he could see the horses in the distant Meadow, noses to the ground, but not even the horses could soothe his soul today. Every pore of his body told him that he had come to the wrong place for comfort this time. He turned around and headed back home. It *was* his home, and he had to make it clear to his mother that he would fight for the house in Powderhorn—for both of them—even if it meant he had to fight *her.*

As soon as he opened the door and entered the kitchen, he could hear Marina's voice. She was on the phone, in the middle of leaving a message. She looked up, and their eyes met. She continued speaking into the phone.

"So I'm calling about my loan application. Please call me, Mr. Holmgren, so we can schedule an inspection. Thank you."

"Who's Holmgren?" Paris asked, not sure what this meant.

"Gordon Holmgren, the loan officer at the bank," Marina said, "I'm not giving up while we still have thirty days."

CHAPTER FIFTEEN

Marina stopped pacing as soon as Gordon Holmgren's car pulled up in front of the house. From the window, Paris could see Mr. Holmgren walk up to the front door. The bank man looked pleased with what he saw. He rang the doorbell.

"How do I look?" Marina asked before answering the door.

"Fine," Paris said with a shrug.

In fact, she looked great. She had pinned up her hair so that loose curls framed her face, and for once, she wasn't wearing bib overalls or jeans. In black slacks and a bright yellow pinstripe blouse, she looked fresh and cool. The bank man, on the other hand, with his clipboard and pen, looked hot and anxious. His short-sleeved shirt suffered from seat-belt compression, and his bow tie of peach and mint summer plaid hung by one sad clip.

"Thanks for coming on such short notice," Marina said, offering her hand.

"Not at all, Mrs. Thibideaux," he said, "I hope you don't mind I'm in my shirtsleeves. I left my jacket in the car."

"Not at all," Marina said, politely indicating that his tie was askew. Embarrassed, he turned away to clip it. She introduced Paris, and they shook hands. Mr. Holmgren had a decent grip, but his hand was sweaty. Marina, however, was not sweaty in the least. Once she opened the door, all the fidgeting and fretting had ceased. Now, she was all ease and grace under pressure, and Paris was (he realized) proud of her. Besides, she looked very pretty.

Marina allowed Mr. Holmgren to take the lead while she and Paris followed him from room to room. It wasn't easy to stay calm, especially when the man paused for a long look at the header with the brace Marina had rigged. A doubtful look came over his face.

"Mrs. Thibideaux, the woodwork and flooring are beautiful, but . . ."

"The header," Marina interjected, "we're prepared to put in a whole new door frame if we have to."

Mr. Holmgren cleared his throat, "I don't know what your contractor has told you, but this brace is not adequate."

At the word "contractor," Paris decided to speak up.

"Oh, we did . . ."

But Marina put her arm around his shoulder and pinched him in such a way that he did not go on. Mr. Holmgren didn't notice.

"We *are* working on it," Marina said. Paris didn't like pretending to have a contractor, but his mother's pinch convinced him to keep his mouth shut.

"You know we have to inspect it before you close up the wall," Holmgren added.

"Of course," Marina said.

In spite of the header, Holmgren liked what she had done in the kitchen, and he said so. Still, it bothered Paris that his mother was fudging the facts. Not only was there no contractor, but she was acting like she knew what to do about the header, when she really didn't. Mr. Holmgren proceeded to write lengthy notes on his clipboard. Paris tried to peek, but the letters were so small that a typewriter could have made them. At last Holmgren stopped and said he was ready to go outside and check the exterior. He examined both the house and the garage from roof to foundation, and didn't have anything nice to say.

"Here is the bottom line, Mrs. Thibideaux. You need new gutters and down spouts, and you'll need to replace the soffits to ventilate the roof. The soffits are rotted, which suggests there may be water damage in the walls. You need to talk to your contractor about getting it done as soon as he's finished with the header."

"I'm planning to," Marina said.

Okay, that's a lie, Paris thought. Why was she trying to hide how much of the work she was doing herself? Why wasn't she proud of it? He was.

"And the header," Holmgren continued, "is an absolute deal breaker. The bank won't approve the loan if we aren't satisfied that it has been properly fixed."

"Yes," Marina confirmed.

"The garage," he went on, "needs paint, certainly, and maybe more. In fact, the cupola, and possibly the whole second floor, may have to go. If—and you've got to understand that it's a big IF—you do these things in the next three to six months, you *may* qualify for a loan."

Paris's heart was pounding. Lose the cupola and maybe the whole loft?

"Thirty days," Marina said.

"Pardon?" Gordon blinked.

"Felix Ermler wants it in thirty days," Marina explained, "or he's going to sell it to another buyer."

"Thirty!" Holmgren exclaimed, his eyebrows doing a little dance over his blue-gray eyes, "Mrs. Thibideaux, it is clear to me that you are working very hard, but . . ."

"But what?"

He hesitated, considering his words carefully.

"Felix Ermler has flipped and re-flipped this property several times already. It's a 'cash cow,' as they say . . ."

"What does that mean?" Paris turned to his mother.

Mr. Holmgren seemed not to notice the boy and addressed Marina.

"You might want to think twice about crossing Felix Ermler," he paused looking very uncomfortable, "It could get ugly."

"If I don't get this loan, Mr. Holmgren, we lose everything. *That's* ugly," Marina said.

Holmgren hated what he was about to say, but it was based on years of doing business in the poorer parts of the city—years of trying to help people like Marina Thibideaux not fall into the traps set by people like Felix Ermler. He had paid a price at the bank for his reputation as a "softie." Lately, he'd been trying to toughen up in hopes of getting a promotion, but his heart went out to Marina, and he was tempted to put her interests ahead of Felix's, even though Felix was a favored client of the bank.

"Mrs. Thibideaux, this is a money game to Mr. Ermler, and it's money *business* to the bank."

Marina's face darkened.

"This house was dead, Mr. Holmgren, and we're bringing it back to life. Why isn't that good enough for the bank?"

Mr. Holmgren opened his mouth, but thought better of it. He knew more than he cared to know about the way Felix Ermler and his colleagues made money in real estate by taking advantage of people's hopes and dreams, not to mention the fundamental human need for shelter.

"We are not moving without a fight," Marina said, looking to Paris. He was glad that she said "we." The bank man didn't look up from his forms when he whispered, "Of course, it's up to you."

Marina walked Mr. Holmgren to his car, and they shook hands. Paris watched from a distance. When his mother finally turned toward the house, she looked very, very tired.

CHAPTER SIXTEEN

A tremendous amount of work was about to take over their lives—that much was clear from Mr. Holmgren's visit. Marina went into the house; she needed some time to herself. Paris seized the opportunity to return to his workshop and try to finish the "belly putter" he was creating for Dan.

Fortunately, Dan had so many putters that he didn't miss the one Paris had taken. The old grip had been removed, probably by Dan, but he hadn't gotten around to scraping off the underlying adhesive, which was old and dried out. Paris scraped off as much as he could and then used sandpaper to smooth the surface. The kickstand that Pete had straightened and polished now fit perfectly into the butt end of the golf club shaft. Paris poured some heavy-duty glue just inside the mouth of the shaft and on the base of the kickstand and put the two together. After wiping away the excess glue, he laid the new and improved putter on the flat surface of his workbench and began to rummage through various boxes and containers. Inside an old hockey bag Paris had retrieved from the trash last winter, he found what he was looking for: an unopened package of "soft grip" hockey tape.

It wasn't a real golf club grip, but it was soft and thick, a mix of cloth and elastic that the package said would "create a custom grip that fits your hand perfectly." When he was finished meticulously wrapping his creation, it was impossible to tell by the look or the feel of it, where the original shaft ended and the kickstand extension began.

Paris selected from his box of decorative pigeon feathers, a speckled pearl gray one and tied it on. Dan would appreciate the feather. Like Paris, he had a quirky affection for pigeons, and respect for their ability to survive in the City in spite of harsh weather, natural predators, and hostile human beings. Dan said, "Pigeons are opportunists. They're noisy and messy and will eat just about anything that falls in front of them, but they're also intelligent creatures that mate for life and live in communities." Paris knew nothing of the mating habits of pigeons, but he had noticed that they would make a home on a narrow ledge as easily as a drafty attic. Having lived in a number of odd and barely habitable places with his mother over the years, Paris identified with their ingenuity and adaptability.

Setting aside the belly putter for an anonymous nighttime delivery, Paris was ready to move on to the next stage of his parade project. He had organized a grand assortment of miscellaneous objects that included a chunk of blown-out truck tire, a rusty watering can, a stack of hubcaps (no two alike), assorted lengths of rebar, some sheet metal, and a roll of chicken wire. But the sorting work was over, so he rolled the bundle of wire to the middle of the room and looked closely at the way it was wound into perfect hexagons. The surface was smooth, but shaping it would require wire cutters and pliers. For the sheet metal, he would need heavy-duty metal shears; and, for the rebar, plenty of hacksaw blades.

He knew now what he wanted to build, although he wasn't sure how he was going to build it, exactly. One thing was certain: with the scale he wanted to achieve and the weight of some of the pieces he wanted to use, the frame would need to be welded together. He told himself that he couldn't ask for Pete's help up front because Pete was too competitive about the Parade, but in his heart he knew that Pete was more generous than competitive. No, the real reason he couldn't ask Pete was his mother. The guys would never agree to let him use the equipment without Marina's permission, and that was not about to happen. First, she would insist there was no time because of the house. Second, if they got beyond that obstacle, she would take one look at the Juice Cart and well—no way. Paris realized that extraordinary ideas sometimes involve extraordinary risk. He would have to "borrow" Pete's equipment without getting caught.

As usual, all this designing and plotting made him hungry. When he left the garage, he had every intention of going into the house and rewarding himself with peanut butter and jelly, but he happened to look up and see something that he couldn't ignore: a pair of sneakers dangling from one of the power lines running from the alley to Max Christenson's house, an example of what Dan called A.I.B, "Alcohol-Induced-Behavior."

"It's the kind of thing that seems brilliant when they're drinkin'," Dan would say, "but really it's just stupid."

Paris grabbed a rake from his garage and tried to snag the sneakers by the laces. They kept swinging about, and the harder he tried, the more tangled the laces became.

"This is not good, this prank," a voice said from somewhere behind him.

Janos stood by his truck with a large coil of yellow electrical cord slung over one shoulder, and a big toolbox at his feet.

Paris was mortified, "I wasn't . . . I mean," he babbled, disengaging the rake.

"You could electrocute yourself. Metal rake and electricity," Janos said, "think about it."

Paris was speechless. The man's eyes were dark and penetrating, by far the most striking feature of his face.

"Why don't you do these things near *your* home? Why do you come here?" Janos asked with disdain.

"I live right there," Paris said, pointing.

"Next door?"

Paris nodded, "I was getting them *down*."

"Oh," Janos said, lifting the heavy toolbox into the truck and getting in, "still, the rake and the wire—pretty stupid."

Paris pointed to the shoes, "Well, *that's* even stupider!"

"I don't debate degrees of stupidity," Janos said, turning the key in the ignition.

Paris approached the truck and said, "I'm Paris!"

Janos rolled up the window. Paris came closer and knocked on it. Janos rolled it down slightly, "Please, I have to go to work."

Paris put his hand through the half-open window and repeated, "I'm Paris."

"Janos," the stern man said, giving a perfunctory handshake, "Now, step away from the truck. I have to go to work."

CHAPTER SEVENTEEN

A shoe whizzed past Billy McNaughton's head. It was his father's way of saying that he did not want to be disturbed.

"You told me to wake you up for work," Billy cried, before slamming everything that stood between him and the outdoors. It was always hell to wake his father after a night of hard drinking, but it would be worse if he didn't try. His father would sleep all day and then be waiting for him with a fist or a belt the next time he came through the door. Not that Harold McNaughton needed an excuse to beat his son. It was practically his only exercise, but somewhere in his alcoholic brain he had a switch that prevented him from going too far, if only to preserve his alarm clock.

Billy found his bike where he'd dropped it the night before, on top of a pile of garbage bags that would never make it to the end of the driveway for pick-up. Among other deficits, Billy's home was lacking a woman's touch. His mother, who had never intended to become a mother on account of her preference for crack, left when he was five. It might have been for the best, as they say, but there was nothing good about it for Billy. She left behind a father and son who fought like wounded animals stuck in a very small cage.

Nevertheless, as much as Billy's father hated his life, he hated the neighbors more. At the top of his list were the immigrants with their foreign food and music and un-American traditions that featured more prominently every year in the Powderhorn Parade. He had lived in Powderhorn all his life, but he had gone sour on the Parade. It reminded him of everything he didn't have, and he blamed everyone but himself for it. In contrast to his father, Billy was drawn to the Parade and watched it with an almost scientific detachment. He was as deprived of family life as any orphan; in fact, between crack and alcohol, you could say he was becoming an orphan, one day at a time. It was a tortuous process, and his only consolation was passing on the hurt. On Parade Day, he watched the moms with their little ones. They always had bottomless bags full of goodies. All day endless supplies of little sandwiches and juice boxes would appear from their baskets and coolers. If he stared at them long enough, someone would offer him a treat, but he always refused. In his prematurely hardened little heart, it felt good to reject their kindness.

Billy was growing into a great bully, a tormentor of small children and a petty thief. This morning anything in the path of his bike was fair game: a Styrofoam sandwich box, a milk carton, a paper cup— pretty much anything that would make a good crunching sound. If he could startle a few birds or cats along the way, that would be especially satisfying. Then, he spotted Paris Thibideaux. As usual, Billy thought, Paris was so completely absorbed in his own fantasy world that he had no idea of his impending doom.

"Hey, Dipstick!" Billy called out.

Instinctively, Paris grabbed a hunk of rope hanging down the side of a telephone pole. It was one of many aids that Paris and other boys before him, had placed around the alley to make it easier to climb up to a roof or get into a tree. He pulled himself and the rope up and out of Billy's reach and pushed off with enough momentum to land on the roof of Dan Torvilson's garage. He ran up one side of the roof and down the other. Then, he vanished!

Billy was on to him; he knew where Paris was headed. He skidded around the corner of Dan's garage and rammed his bike into the Torvilson's gate. The delicate repair job fell apart, and the pigeon feather fell to the ground. Billy kicked aside the gate and marched into the yard yelling, "Come out, you chicken-shit!"

"What is going on?" Helen cried, appearing at her back door.

"Take it easy, Ma," Dan said, rising from the couch to take a stand in the middle of the porch.

"Get off my putting green," he said, mustering something of the former Marine within.

"Make Paris come out and fight," Billy demanded.

"It's time to go home, Billy," Dan said, beginning to cough.

"Bite me!" Billy sneered, pulling the flagpole out of the green and waving it over his head.

Dan glowered, "Don't tempt me, boy!"

Billy lowered the flag and pointed at him, "I'm not afraid of you!"

The next thing Billy knew was that Tommy had grabbed him by the collar, relieved him of the flag, and proceeded to march him out of the yard and into the alley. Billy kicked and flailed, spitting and cursing every step of the way.

Dan recognized in Billy a strain of viciousness that was often a kid's response to a hard-handed father. He had grown up with Harold McNaughton, and it pained him to see that Harold was passing on the home life that had made him such a reckless youth. Where Paris and Billy were headed—if left to their own devices—was a very bad place, and Dan wanted very much to prevent it.

"I'm gonna get that kid," Billy swaggered, "and you can't stop me."

"Get going, Bill, and cool off," Tommy said, releasing him.

"Later, Paris, when your grandpas aren't around," he yelled as he picked up his bike and took off down the alley.

"Come in the house, now," Helen said, touching Dan's arm lightly.

"I'll be right in, Ma. Go ahead," Dan said, patting her hand.

Tommy replaced the flag in its proper place on the green. He glanced at the tree, nodded to Dan, and followed his aunt inside. As soon as the screen door closed, Dan looked up and said, "You're playing awfully close to the edge, don't ya think?"

"*He* is," Paris countered, "He's always after me!"

"I can see that," Dan said.

He moved to the sofa and pulled a cigarette from his shirt pocket. He was short of breath, but he liked to have a cigarette in his hand when he had something important to say, even if he didn't light it.

"There," he said, settling himself, "where was I?"

"Playing it close to the edge," Paris said.

"Ah, yes, I was about to impart wisdom," Dan said, "You know, Paris, I grew up in this neighborhood," Dan said, suddenly seized by a hoarse cough that made every word sound painful, "I'm trying to pass on some . . ."

Paris couldn't stand it. He dropped out of the tree and sprinted out of the yard, away from Dan and his cancer, away from whatever Dan was trying to pass on. He wasn't ready for it. Dan realized that he'd messed up the moment. It had come upon him so suddenly— the realization that he *ought* to try to intervene for Paris's sake. But his reflexes weren't what they used to be. His body had let him down, and he didn't have the breath to call after Paris and start over. All he could do was lean back on the cushions and close his eyes.

"You okay, Danny?" Helen asked through the screen door.

"I'm just gonna take a little nap out here, okay Ma?" Dan said.

Helen lifted his legs on to the sofa and covered them with a light blanket. Dan pulled his cap down over his face, "Thanks, Ma."

CHAPTER EIGHTEEN

Turning his back on Dan was something Paris never expected to do. He couldn't believe that he had done it. But something had seized up inside him. He couldn't stand another minute of Dan's sickness and that hacking cough that sounded like it might rip him apart. He could choose not to face Dan, but he found out quickly that he couldn't run away from himself. He was tired of being afraid of Billy, and ashamed of running away all the time. And yet, here he was, doing it again.

He entered the barn, seeking only to hide. There was an event in the old arena that day, and most of the stalls were empty. He had barely enough time to hide before he heard the familiar clop of horseshoes striking the concrete floor. A man's gruff voice echoed throughout the barn. Paris could only see his legs. He had on fancy riding boots streaked with dirt, and his pants had rips in the knees. He spoke harshly to the horse.

"You're a regular beast today, aren't you? Cost me a good pair of britches," he muttered, "I should sell you to this stable so you can spend your days giving pony rides to idiots."

The horse skittered and shied in response to his rough handling. The man left her still saddled, frustrated, and loose in the stall. His boots struck the hard concrete as he walked briskly out of the barn. Paris could feel the heat and smell the sweat still clinging to the horse's body. He felt sorry for her. Restless and thirsty, she thrust her muzzle into the water bucket to cool off. Paris stood up slowly. The next thing he knew, he was looking up at the underside of a massive gray head on top of a long thick neck. The horse had a broad muscular chest and long powerful legs. The hooves looked big enough to crush rocks. Paris flattened himself against the wall, and the horse lowered its head and lunged at him, striking him in the belly. It was like getting hit with a bowling ball. He gasped and held himself up out of pure terror of being trampled.

He tried to reach the stall door, but the horse nipped at his arm and forced him to retreat. In his agitation, the horse scraped his hindquarters against the walls, stomping and fidgeting and making a horrible racket punctuated by snorts and kicks that Paris feared would crush him. The horse had set the barn astir with hundreds of wings fanning the air, and sharp little nails and claws gripping and slipping among the rafters.

Paris believed that in a minute he would be too tired and weak to protect himself. The horse's black golf-ball eyes rolled back, and his ears flattened against his head. The worst seemed to be happening. His legs were melting; his knees gave out. The horse reared up and towered over him. A sharp cry escaped from his throat, and he lost his grip on the world. He was flying. There was no pain, no light. Just weightlessness, silence, and a dark curtain fell heavily over him.

CHAPTER NINETEEN

With the opening of his eyes his other senses awakened: first, he tasted salt—blood in his mouth—and felt the swelling of his lips where his teeth had cut into them. Next, he felt the strong arms and rough hands of a man carrying him. It wasn't the riding britches man. This man was bigger, and his shoulder was like a hard pillow. Paris's head lay heavily against it. The man's face was only inches away; his chin was scratchy; his neck smelled of soap and sweat and saw dust. Most extraordinary was the scar on his neck, pinkish and smooth, extending from just above his collar. Paris thought he had seen it before; it looked like a serious burn. The man lowered him to the ground, and cradling the boy's head in his hands, he lowered it carefully to the cold, hard floor. Suddenly, Paris found himself face-to-face with Janos Kovac.

Lying on the barn floor, Paris thought the world looked tilted as though it had fallen off its axis. The gray horse stood like an apparition, still snorting and blowing, his coat glistening with sweat. Janos went to him and spoke gently. The barn critters in the rafters kept up a racket, but Janos's voice was soothing and low.

"Yes, yes. You are all right. Quiet now. Look how you stir up everybody."

Janos began to do the work that the other man should have done, taking off the saddle and bridle, brushing and combing and calming, and he began to sing. In a deep soothing voice, a song as sweet as a lullaby, but in words Paris could not understand. His song calmed the whole barn.

"Okay boy," he said, picking up one foot at a time, and cleaning them with a hoof pick, "you are beautiful, and you know it—strong legs, big lungs, good back. They're going to ruin you, though," he said, "if they don't treat you with more respect, eh? Well, I wish you luck with that."

Janos, Paris murmured to himself. There was something about his broad back and the set of his shoulders that inspired a mix of awe and dread in the flustered boy. When Janos turned around, his eyes were full of disapproval. Paris braced himself for a scolding, but Janos just shook his head and walked out of the barn. Paris got to his feet and, unsteadily, made for the barn doors. In the late afternoon sun, everything went white, and the ground came up fast. Behind him, a stern voice pulled him up short.

"Go slow or you faint."

Janos was leaning against the barn door, no sign of compassion in his dark countenance.

"You shouldn't be in there, boy."

"It wasn't my fault. That horse was in the wrong stall," Paris said defensively.

"No, *you* were in the wrong," Janos said, coming toward him, "You are lucky they are all busy with a horse show today, or you would be . . ."

"I know," Paris moaned, "I was . . ."

"Stupid. And dangerous. Not just for you. For horse! He can hurt himself. Did you think of that?" Janos demanded.

Paris squinted up at him pathetically. With the sun behind him, Janos seemed particularly ominous. His forearms had bronzed from working in the sun, but they were marked by scars—smaller but otherwise like the ones on his neck. Their pattern was haphazard and crude. Paris felt small and foolish before this man whose life, he guessed, must have been very hard. He stared at the ground and at the man's work boots, scuffed and dusty and planted firmly in his path. Paris's head was spinning.

"I should turn you in," Janos said.

"No, please," Paris begged, "I'm sorry."

"Don't pee your pants. You get a second chance," Janos said flatly, "but don't push your luck."

The parental tone of his own voice surprised him, and Janos could see that it surprised the boy, too. But Paris was mostly embarrassed. He thought that Janos saw him only as a child, and a stupid child at that.

"What's the matter, you feel sick?" Janos asked without a shred of sympathy.

Paris nodded miserably.

"Good! Feel it! Learn from it!" Janos said coolly, "I have to pack up now."

Paris watched Janos take off his tool belt and stow his tools in the big silver box. He didn't just toss them in the way Pete might. He handled the tools with care, and Paris admired the orderly interior of the toolbox, so much like the beautiful machines he had seen that first day in the back of Janos's truck.

"You go straight home or I tell your mother everything," Janos said, as he got into the truck. Paris watched the truck drive away and then reluctantly aimed his aching body toward home. As he walked, a chill came over him. He looked down at his shaking hands, crusted with dirt and dried blood. He had acquired quite a few scratches and a couple of splinters, too. His bottom lip was swollen where he'd bitten it. And he was going to have to face his mother.

CHAPTER TWENTY

Janos could have given the boy a lift home, but he drove past him. *Let him walk and think*, he said to himself. The truth was, Janos was as shaken as Paris by what had just happened, but for different reasons. He blamed his hands for bringing back memories he had struggled to forget. They were memories laden with emotion that had the power to move him involuntarily; and, sensory memories that drew him to the terrified boy, crumpled in a heap, half in and half out of the stall. He secured the horse first. Then he scooped up the boy and laid him down gently away from danger. How many times had he done this sort of thing during the war? The first time he had tried to save a child, she had fallen apart like a broken doll. She was only a baby, and her life slipped right through his fingers. They had been hiding in the basement when the black-uniforms swept through the village. Dragged into the light of an impossibly sunny day, they were shot down in their own back yard.

He looked at his hands gripping the steering wheel now as he drove home from work. The missing flesh of his hand where the bullet passed through, shattered her skull, and lodged in his shoulder where she had buried her face in terror. Same hands. They were a workman's hands, his father's hands, except for the disfigurement. Such a man of true faith, his father was. Janos wished he could be more like him, but war had made that impossible. It was hard to be still breathing, still occupied with the mundane operations of living while his family lay in their graves.

"You want to lie down with the dead, Janos," his father had said when the unrest first began, "but there is no place for the living in the bone yard. The dead don't want our aggravation. We have mixed and married for generations here. We are proof that it can be done!"

Janos wanted to believe that the Muslims and Christians could do better than to repeat their bloody history. Then came the hour, maybe two, that Janos had truly lain with the dead, pretending to be one of them, listening to the shooting and the screaming of his neighbors. When it finally ended, Janos dragged himself back into the basement, and began what he considered his non-life. He survived, he fought, he saved other people's children, he came to America, but he could love nothing and no one any more. As far as he was concerned, Death was playing a cruel joke on him by denying him. And yet, the body acts out of habit even when the heart is broken and the mind can no longer imagine anything good coming from humanity.

CHAPTER TWENTY ONE

When Janos got home, Max and Two-Ton were waiting for him in the driveway.

"Here's the chair I told you about. What do you think?" Max said, proudly indicating an old armchair that he called his "lazy boy." He sat down in the chair and demonstrated its reclining properties.

"Looks good. I buy it from you," Janos said reaching for his wallet.

"No!" Max insisted, "Solveigh already bought a new one. Take it off my hands, I'll be grateful."

"Okay, thanks," Janos said, "I take it."

Janos tilted the chair backwards and prepared to push it up the stairs from underneath, hoping it would slide easily over the outdoor-carpeting. Suddenly, Two-Ton lunged for the chair and carried off the seat cushion.

"Two-Ton, drop it!" Max commanded, but the dog bolted across the alley toward Pete and Blossum's place. Janos scowled in silence. His attitude darkened even more when Pete and Blossum returned the cushion a moment later.

"Hey, man, you lose somethin'?" the short stocky one said with a chuckle, "how you doing? I'm Pete. This is Blossum. We got a minute, if you need . . ."

"No, thanks," Janos said, snatching back the seat of his chair, and returning to the business of moving the chair upstairs. Pete thrust his hands into his pockets and looked to Max, who simply shrugged.

"That's Janos Kovac, just moved into the apartment," Max said confidentially.

"Likes to be left alone, huh," Blossum concluded.

Pete shook his head, "You can't know that. Maybe, he's shy."

"Please. I am right here. You can talk to me. I am not shy," Janos said pointedly, "I am busy."

Pete and Blossum nodded respectfully to Max and headed back across the alley. Janos started up the stairs with the chair. A piece of hanging fabric tripped him up, though, and the sharp edge of the banister caught him as he backed down to the bottom. He cried out in pain. To his consternation, someone laughed and let out a sharp whistle.

"Yo, Marina, wait up!" a woman called out, and he realized that the laugh and the whistle were not for him. At first sight, her bright pink dress gave her the appearance of a bubble floating up the alley. The person she was hailing, Marina, had stopped at the edge of Max's driveway. She wore jeans and work boots and had a small Thermos clipped to her belt. Her dark hair hung in a thick braid down the middle of her back.

"Hi, Randi," she said to the Buoyant One.

Randi held out a white paper bag, "Have some popcorn?"

"Thanks," Marina said.

"Keep me company. I'm playing hide and seek with the kids."

"Where are they?" Marina asked, looking around.

"Who?" Randi asked blankly.

"The kids!" Marina exclaimed.

"Just kidding," Randi laughed, "I know exactly where they went, but I don't plan to find them for another half hour. One of the perks of being It."

Now, as they munched popcorn, they turned and took in the awkward figure hugging a Laz-E-Boy at the bottom of the stairs. Marina smiled, and her vitality made him feel old. He picked up the base of the chair, the heaviest and most awkward part, and every muscle in his back rebuked him for turning down the help of his neighbors. But like a schoolboy, he would not back down in front of the women.

"Go for it, big guy!" Randi exclaimed gleefully.

Janos pretended to be on another planet, but his vanity brought a fresh supply of extra blood to his face.

"Come on, Randi. The man's trying to concentrate," Marina admonished her friend.

Janos stared at the ground, contemplating the bolts and upholstery tacks that had fallen from the chair and now littered the driveway. As he stooped to gather them up, the women lingered, eating popcorn and watching him like he was a circus act. Feeling doomed, he dropped the bolts and tacks into his shirt pocket. They pressed against his chest painfully when he lifted the chair, but even if they had drawn blood he would not stop now. Stifling a groan, he gained the first three stairs, and the next several, and the last few. At the top, his arms gave out, and the unwieldy thing crashed, taking him down with it.

Following the sound of their muffled laughter, he turned. They were walking on at last. Without looking back, Marina waved good-by to him over her shoulder. She didn't even have to turn around to know that he was watching. He felt flushed like when he was a little boy, and his sisters teased him. The women separated. Randi went on alone, but Marina turned into the yard next door and went into the house—Paris's house.

CHAPTER TWENTY TWO

Janos reached for a bottle of vodka and a glass he kept in the freezer. He pulled a kitchen chair out on to the balcony and sat down. The first shot went down easily; he poured another. Next door a screen door whined on its hinges.

"Pa - ris! Dinner!"

Janos sipped and watched Marina go to the alley and call out again. She was a commanding little figure with a flat, boyish gait.

"Yoohoo, Marina! I was hoping I'd catch you," another woman called to her.

"Hi, Helen. You look so nice!" Marina exclaimed. The older woman touched the lace collar of her dress self-consciously.

"Oh," Helen said, "I just have a meeting with my ladies at the Veterans hall. They want to do something for Danny."

"How is he?" Marina inquired.

"As good as . . . you know," she sighed, "and how's your boy?"

Marina brightened, "I was just calling him to supper. Have you seen him?"

"No, dear, I haven't," Helen replied.

"Oh, well," Marina shrugged, "he'll come home when he's hungry. I hope it's soon, though. We need to talk about those gutters," she added looking up at the rusting hunks of metal hanging from her roof. Helen looked skeptical.

"You going to do those yourself?" she asked.

"Looks that way," Marina said.

"I sure do admire you, Marina, but be careful! It's probably rotten up there," she said earnestly.

Maybe, it was the mellowing effect of the vodka, but Janos was drawn to the sound of women's voices talking about ordinary things. He downed another shot, and welcomed the haze that was beginning to envelop his aching head.

"Dan don't look so good today," Helen said, "could you maybe check on him later? I won't be long, maybe an hour or so."

"Sure, Helen. No problem," Marina said, glancing at her watch and looking around for her son.

"I just don't like to leave him all alone," Helen added.

"It'll be fine, Helen," Marina said. She was worried about her son, too. He should be home by now.

"Oh! And don't let him know I asked you," Helen said over her shoulder as she hurried away, "you know how he hates a fuss."

"Don't worry!" Marina said good-naturedly, "Go, go!"

As soon as Helen was gone, the smile left Marina's face. She crossed the yard again and called out into the alley.

"Pa - ris! Paris Thibideaux! Dinner!"

Janos knew why Paris was late, but he wished he didn't. Like a hermit crab diving into his shell, he withdrew into his house.

CHAPTER TWENTY THREE

Paris needed an extra block just to clear his head and consider how he was going to explain his injuries to his mother. Even so, when he reached his own back yard, all he knew was that Truth was not an option if he ever wanted to go to the park again. Whatever he came up with would not include the horse, the barn, or Janos.

"Paris! What happened to you?" Marina gasped, as soon as he came through the back door, "Have you been fighting? Oh, my God, you've been fighting!"

Startled, he decided to roll with it.

"Sorry . . ." Paris began. His mother's greatest fear, he knew, was that he would turn into a neighborhood "hoodlum." That was her word for a kid gone wrong. She pulled him to the sink, turned on the cold water, and started dabbing his cheeks with a wet dishtowel, inspecting his hands.

"Who was it?" she asked, "Was it Billy? Of course, it was Billy."

"Ow! That hurts!" Paris cried as she held his hands under the stream of cold water.

"I'm sorry, honey. This will keep the swelling down," she said, running her cold wet hands over his face, and pressing her cool fingers on his eyelids. The cold water made his fingers ache, but he kept his mouth shut.

"What in the world were you fighting about?" she demanded, drying him off.

"Ow! You're rubbing my skin off!" Paris cried. One minute she was all sweetness and sympathy, and the next she was the Monster Mommy, snarling and sarcastic. She started rummaging through drawers and cupboards until she found a plastic bag suitable to make an ice pack. As she emptied an ice tray noisily on the counter, she fumed, "Don't lie to me, Paris. What were you fighting about?"

"Nothing!" Paris insisted, "He just hates me. He hates everybody." That was true enough.

"Nothing!" she exclaimed, as she slammed the ice bag against his face, "Your lip is blowing up like a balloon."

He nodded weakly.

"I'm calling Harold McNaughton . . ." she declared, reaching for the phone.

"No! He'll kill me! Mom, please, stay out of it. It'll be okay."

"Okay? O-K?" she repeated like she was stuck.

Paris's thoughts were tumbling around like lottery balls. He grabbed one out of the air.

"You should see *him*!" he exclaimed, boldly tossing his soul to the devil.

"Oh! I see," she said, "So now you're a hoodlum just like Billy! I suppose Harold McNaughton will be calling ME next."

"Mom, I'm not like Billy," Paris protested.

"I don't have time for this, Paris," she said, folding her arms across her chest, "you fight in the streets, you come home bloody. This is not what I work fifty hours a week for. She slammed her fist on the counter.

Desperate to simply put an end to the cascade of lies and innuendos, Paris followed his wildest impulse yet. He hugged his mother. And once he was in his mother's arms, he had to admit it felt good. Marina was so surprised that all she could do was hug

85

him back. He smiled up at her with his dirty, battered boy's face, and her heart melted.

"Oh, let's get you cleaned up," she said kindly, "we can talk about the rest later."

Yes! Paris thought.

CHAPTER TWENTY FOUR

After sleeping the fitful sleep of one who has narrowly escaped disaster, Paris awakened with a noble and daring idea—never mind that he could get killed doing it. It came to him by way of a vivid dream in which he relived the moment when Janos rescued him from the horse. In the dream Paris kept trying to say something terribly important, but he couldn't find his voice. No matter how hard he tried, he was mute; and Janos looked at him with a mixture of pity and contempt. He awakened from this dream unsettled and anxious. As often happens with dreams, the details began to fade quickly; but, the feelings worked and worked on him. What was he trying to say? Again and again, the words rose to his lips like bubbles and evaporated before he could utter them. And then it came to him: the words weren't as important as the impulse he felt to say them. He needed to thank Janos as he had failed to do at the time of the incident.

But how does a boy thank a man who, from his manner, makes it clear that he places little value on the exchange of words or sentiment? What might hold more meaning for him? Paris suddenly remembered *the camera*. He would get back Janos's stolen camera.

It was simple and brilliant. All he had to do was sneak up to Billy's house, find and snatch the camera, and get out alive. Of course, sensible people avoided the McNaughton house. There was a rumor, mostly spread by Billy, that the property was booby-trapped against intruders. Somewhere along the foundation, there was supposed to be an open window that was Billy's secret passage in and out of the house. He liked to brag that he could come and go whenever he wanted because, as he put it, "Even my old man's afraid to go down to the basement."

Billy hinted that it was like a torture chamber. Paris doubted it, but to be on the safe side, he prepared like a commando on a deadly mission. He took his fishing rod, which was sturdy and had plenty of fresh line still on the reel even though the hook was in a tangle that Paris had to cut free and retie. He clipped a small flashlight to a belt loop on his jeans. Next, he taped the ankles of his jeans with duct tape so they wouldn't snag on anything or allow varmints to munch on his bare legs. He put a bandanna around his neck that could be pulled up to protect his face, and he pulled his baseball cap down low over his forehead. Into his back pants pocket he slipped his penknife.

It was early in the morning, cloudy and cool. He had to grit his teeth to keep them from chattering, and it wasn't because it was chilly. The smell of the McNaughton place reached him as the yard's forbidding landscape came into view. In the middle stood an old stove with the oven door mangled and hanging by one hinge. There was no lawn, only dirt, trash and broken beer bottles. Garbage cans and trash bags stood with their contents overflowing. He pulled up the bandanna to cover his nose and mouth, but it wasn't much help. He had one last chance to reconsider. Billy's back yard loomed before him—he was at that point beyond which no boy goes unless he has to.

Paris dropped to a crouch. The windows and the back door of the house were open, and Paris could hear Billy and his father arguing. He realized with some relief that as long as he could hear their raised voices, they probably couldn't hear him. He took a deep breath, counted to three, and ran for the stove. From there it was only a few feet to the house. He could hear Billy and Harold more clearly now.

"I'm gonna beat that money outa you, you sneaky little . . ."

"Get off me!" Billy choked, "It's mine!"

Harold let out a triumphant laugh, and Billy cried out in pain, "No! Give it back!"

Paris ran from the shelter of the stove, keeping his head down and his knees bent. Suddenly, he was face down in the dirt with the wind knocked out of him. He had tripped and landed right on top of the fishing pole. Luckily, it wasn't broken. Quickly, he rose to his hands and knees and power-crawled the remaining distance to the house. Through the grimy glass of a cellar window, he could just make out the water heater, a tall blue cylinder. Inching along the foundation of the house under cover of thickly overgrown weeds, he came upon Billy's secret window. It was completely unhinged, leaning against the opening into the basement.

Slowly and silently, Paris lifted the window and carefully moved it aside. He unclipped his flashlight and aimed the beam of light into the gloom below. Through the cobwebs, he couldn't see much until something glinted in the dark. Yes! It was the camera sitting on top of an upended garbage can. It was well out of arm's reach, but that was the genius of bringing the fishing pole. He squeezed his upper body through the small window opening and, with the flashlight in one hand and the fishing pole in the other, began to maneuver the fishhook into position. It was clumsy work, and Paris felt like he was sawing himself in half on the splintery edge of the windowsill.

Harold McNaughton roared, "I want all of it!"

Billy cried out again, and Paris knew that he was in pain, but relief that his enemy couldn't be in two places at once outweighed his natural inclination toward pity. He put the flashlight into his mouth to free up his hands and eased himself a little further into the basement. He heard his T-shirt rip and felt the cloth give way under his arm. One more shirt, his mother had warned, and he was going to be wearing a garbage bag with holes cut out for his head and arms.

Trying to aim the flashlight in his mouth was a coordination challenge. He seemed to be sending the light beam everywhere but where he needed it to go. That was because his eyes were darting all over the place, and where his eyes went, so went the flashlight. Once he figured that out, things began to make sense, but he was so stretched over the ledge that if he fell in, he would fall on his head; and if the fall didn't kill him, Billy certainly would.

With visions of Billy's fists coming down like hammers on his head, he pushed for that last millimeter standing between him and the camera strap. His heart felt like a bullfrog in his chest, but at last he hooked it! Lifting it gingerly, he began reeling it in. The camera dragged along the top of the garbage can and swept a heap of bicycle chains to the floor. He stopped breathing, closed his eyes, and listened. Nothing else moved. Doggedly, he reeled in the camera until it he could lift it free of the window frame. Sitting with his back against the side of the house, he put his head through the neck strap and breathed deeply. It was quiet. Too quiet. No voices. Where was Billy now?

Paris willed himself up on his knees. He was no longer cold; he was sweating, burning up in fact. He got to his feet and made a run for the stove in the middle of the yard. Suddenly Billy burst out of the house, his nose and knuckles bloody.

"Paris!" he shouted, "you prick!"

Like an absurd tourist with the camera hanging around his neck, Paris stopped in the middle of the yard.

"Drop that camera," Billy roared, "and I won't kill you!"

Paris broke into a run. Billy leaped off the back stoop and charged after him. If it hadn't been such a rough morning in the McNaughton household, he might have caught Paris, but in the interest of staying alive, Paris found more speed than he had ever known. And Billy had the bad luck to trip over a garbage bag that brought him down. Paris ran straight up the alley and into Mrs. Vang's yard.

"Paris!" her little granddaughter exclaimed, clapping.

"Shhhhh!" Mrs. Vang put a finger to her lips. She could tell that the boy was on the run. He vaulted over the compost bin, climbed the chain link fence, and was on the roof of the neighboring garage just as Billy came in.

"You! Out!" Mrs. Vang was on her feet and brandishing a rake.

Billy tried to dodge the old lady, but the little girl screamed when she saw Billy's bloody hands and face. Billy knew where Paris was headed, and how he could still catch him. He ducked back into the alley and went straight for Pete's Forest of Lawn Mowers. He caught sight of Paris scrambling over an old John Deere 56 ride-on mower. Billy picked up a rock and threw a fastball at Paris's head. It glanced off of Paris's ear, but hit hard enough to stop Paris in his tracks. His hand flew to his ear and came back sticky with blood. Immediately ahead lay the rusting hulk of a blue Pontiac LeMans, its wheels almost completely sunken into the earth. Paris climbed up on the hood and went on to the roof with Billy closing in fast.

"Gimme the camera or I'll smash your face," he growled. The boys faced each other, gasping for breath. Suddenly, Billy dove for Paris and latched on to his ankle.

"Ahh-oww!" Paris cried, as he lost his balance and came down hard on the roof of the car. Billy held him fast and punched Paris's thigh while also trying to hook his fingers in the neck strap of the camera. Paris had never had to really fight before, having always been able to outrun and outthink Billy. But the ache in his head and the ringing in his ear left no room in his brain for reason. He was acting on instinct now. The fishing rod seemed to come alive in his hand as he whipped it across Billy's face. THWACK! It struck his fleshy cheek and left a dark welt. THWIP! He hit him again, and Billy fell to the ground, cursing and clutching his face.

Paris looked down at Billy, his chest heaving, his hand still tingling with the impact of the rod on Billy's face. He leaped off the car and was about to dive under the Hoistabus when he heard Blossum's voice like thunder.

"Stop, both of you! You don't do this here. This is my place!" Blossum bellowed as he hurried toward them from the garage with Pete scurrying to keep up.

Billy lunged for Paris, but missed. Paris threw himself under the Hoistabus. He had got what he wanted from Billy; now, all he wanted was to go home. Billy tried to dive under the bus after Paris.

WHACK! Blossum's heavy blacksmith tongs struck the side of the Hoistabus and made a colossal dent. Billy curled up on the ground like a slug. Pete gave Blossum a quizzical look.

"I'll fix that later," Blossum said apologetically, pointing to the dent, and then he addressed the boys, one of whom was still under the bus, "What are you thinking?"

Silence.

"Speak up!" Pete added.

Even more silence.

"Any thinking going on at all? I don't think so."

Billy tried to stand up.

WHACK! Blossum hit the side of the Hoistabus once more, and Billy sat down.

"No thinkin' at all, Blossum," Pete agreed, "no sign of intelligent life in these two at the moment."

Paris seized the opportunity of Billy's being subdued to slide out from under the Hoistabus and sprint home.

Blossum called after him, "Not good, Paris! Disappointing!"

Pete put a hand on Billy's shoulder, "End it here, Billy, how 'bout it?"

Billy got up and backed away from the men. When he got far enough away, he released a bloody gob of spit in their direction. Then he turned and slouched toward home. He wasn't in a hurry now, and this wasn't the end of anything.

CHAPTER TWENTY FIVE

Once inside the house, Paris locked the door behind him and collapsed. For a moment, the kitchen took a spin around his head as he leaned against the solid door. He had beat Billy at his own game, but it had cost him plenty. His ear had begun to throb where the rock had ricocheted off of his skull, and blood oozed thickly from the wound. When he opened his eyes, the kitchen had stopped spinning. He went to the sink and wiped away the blood and dirt with a wet paper towel.

He eased himself into a chair at the kitchen table and opened the camera case. He held the prize of the day in his hands, something that belonged to Janos. To his delight, it hadn't been damaged at all. It was one of those tough old things that never die. It had black leather over a silver casing, and it was thin but felt heavy in his hand. A word that he couldn't pronounce was etched into the silver, and like all of Janos's tools, it had been maintained beautifully. He wondered if there was any film left in it, but he had no idea how to find out. He held the camera up to his eye.

The image was blurred until he started turning the lens. The refrigerator came into focus. He pressed the button, but nothing happened. With his thumb, he pressed a lever that swung around the corner of the camera casing. He did it again, and a number in the little window advanced. When he let go, the lever snapped back. Cool! Impulsively he turned the camera on himself and pressed the button with his fingertip. Snap! He tried to snap another, but the camera was locked up again. He repeated what he had done before with the lever and watched the number change. Aiming the camera at himself once more—this time he was more thoughtful about his pose—and snap again! It was such a satisfying and precise sound.

It wasn't even nine o'clock yet, but he had been up for several exhausting hours. He needed to go back to bed for a while. To his surprise, he found his mother curled up on the couch in the living room, still in her work clothes. Sometimes after a long night, she didn't bother trying to make it upstairs. Clutched to her chest was a black and white composition book that was the record of her work on the house. It had absorbed a fair amount of coffee and grease, and it had a swollen look from having been left out in the rain more than once. Between the bound pages she had stuffed loose sheets, larger drawings that she had folded to fit. A couple of rubber bands held it all together.

Paris crept closer to sit and watch her sleep. In the act of bending, he began to feel the new aches and cuts that he had acquired in the quest for the camera. All of the blows and tumbles he had taken over the past few days had left him so bruised and battered that he felt and moved like an old man, but at least the ringing in his ear had stopped.

He and Marina hadn't talked about the house since Mr. Holmgren's visit when she had lied about having a contractor. He was proud of what they were doing *without* the help of a contractor, and it bothered him that she had tried to cover it up like she was ashamed of it. On the other hand, as he looked at her now, lying there so exhausted with work and worry, his disappointment no longer seemed important. She had brought them along this far; maybe he should trust her more, and not less. Bathed in morning light, she looked so peaceful, lying on her side with a rolled up sweatshirt under her cheek. Her thick hair was loose, and the longer strands collected in a pool of curls resting on her neck and shoulders. She looked younger. She used to wear her hair down all the time when he was little, and he used to love burying his hands and face in it.

The play of the light accentuated the waves ands folds of Marina's hair and brought out the golden tones of her brown skin. Paris lifted the camera to his eye and brought her image into focus. It was like looking back in time to see her this way, and yet he could also see that long hours and worry were wearing her out. He took another picture, and then one more. Quietly, he ascended the stairs, and hid the camera in the back of his closet. Regardless of his weariness, getting the camera was only the beginning. Now, he had to figure out exactly how to give it back to Janos.

CHAPTER TWENTY SIX

Paris understood that a gift of kindness deserves a proper response. He hadn't learned this from his mother. She suspected selfish motives behind most charity because Life had taught her that anyone in a position to help, also has the power to cheat or betray you. Her solution was to do everything herself so that no one got the chance to deceive her. Consequently, she worked practically every waking hour, and she didn't have to say thank-you very often.

Paris was not like his mother. He was a boy. By nature a risk taker, he was just beginning to grasp the foolishness of hiding in an empty stall. If Janos had not put himself in harm's way, Paris now recognized, the consequences could have been deadly. That was the nature of his obligation to Janos and, unlike his mother, Paris was eager to honor it.

He gave a lot of thought to when and how he would return the camera because he wanted the gesture to mean something to Janos in a way that, so far, chance conversations had not. He didn't want to remain anonymous, as with his other good deeds in the neighborhood. And it wasn't enough to merely drop off the camera like a pizza order. He was determined to deliver it in a way that would surprise and gladden Janos, because he seemed to be a man in need of a reason to smile.

Paris waited until after midnight before stepping out of his bedroom window and climbing down the trellis. The night was unusually still, and the alley light seemed to melt into the dreary, starless sky. It threw an unpleasant buttery glare over Max's driveway and into the big maple that stood before Janos's porch.

Paris clung to the shadows and moved carefully, protective of stiff joints and aching muscles from the day's combat with Billy. On top of the scrapes and bumps he had sustained in the barn the day before, he knew, these new injuries were going to bloom by morning into a whole new set of bruises and swellings that he would have to hide from his mother. But that wasn't important right now.

With the camera hung around his neck, Paris arrived at the base of the stairs leading to Janos's apartment. It was still oddly quiet. No sirens; not even an alley cat was stirring. Paris stepped carefully out of the shadows and began climbing the stairs. The alley light gave an eerie sheen to his skin that made him feel strangely masked, but with every creak of the old wooden steps, he wished he could drop the camera right there and run home. But he hadn't risked the wrath of Billy McNaughton only to be put off by a few squeaky boards. He had a plan for where to place the camera, and he had to stick to it.

At the top of the stairs, he paused before crossing in front of Janos's kitchen window. The inside of the house was dark and still. Paris moved to the porch rail and began looking for a branch on which the hang the camera. He put one leg on the outside of the railing and leaned out. This placed him inches from the edge of the roof, but he knew this tree well enough to move confidently. He parted the leaves and hung the camera. When the leaves fell back into place, the camera was visible but not obvious. Stepping back over the railing, Paris took a moment to savor his accomplishment. Now, all that remained was to return home like a tired soldier, which is how he felt now that his mission was over.

He moved stealthily toward the stairs, but something made him pause before the kitchen window and peer inside. So this was how a man lived alone. There was a small table and a folding chair right in front of him. The place had the look of a warehouse with boxes scattered about, and along the walls instead of furniture, Janos kept the larger tools Paris had seen on the day Janos moved in. And there on a coat hook was Janos's tool belt with a cordless drill neatly holstered.

Suddenly a light went on in the far end of the apartment. Paris dropped to his hands and knees, keeping his head below the windowsill. Then the kitchen light went on, spilling out on the porch as well. Paris heard the clink of glass and the gush of running water. He pictured Janos drinking the water and then coming out for air. And there he would see Paris cowering like a thief. A few agonizing seconds passed, and finally the kitchen light went out. Paris scurried down the stairs (creaks be damned!), ran across the driveway, and into the shadow of his house. He knew he was safe.

His heart was racing and he was still breathing heavily, but slowly a grin began to spread from ear to ear. With one action he had both repaid Janos and antagonized Billy. One debt was paying back a kindness, and the other was simply payback.

CHAPTER TWENTY SEVEN

Paris woke up with a face like a prizefighter who's gone ten rounds with a gorilla. His ear looked twice its normal size, his arms bore scratches and scrapes, and his fingers were swollen like little sausages. On his thigh, hidden by his shorts, was an especially ugly bruise like a small eggplant where Billy had pummeled him. Marina was sitting at the table eating cornflakes when he came down. She looked at him and gasped, "Oh, Paris, your face! And your ear! I don't remember you being so swollen."

Just the kind of scrutiny he didn't want this morning.

"I'm fine, Mom," he said, avoiding her eyes that clearly wanted to know more. He carried his bowl of cereal to the back door where he ate and stood with his back to her, watching with envy as his neighbors worked on their parade preparations. Stilt-walkers paced the alley like long-legged birds, and jugglers practiced in Dan's driveway. Pete and Blossum were shut up in their garage with their parade secrets, but in the course of an hour their frequent arguments forced one or the other of them outdoors to cool off. Children created a supply line of paints, fabrics, pipe cleaners, crepe paper, and glue for floats and costumes from one yard to the next.

"The whole neighborhood is working on the parade," Paris said, longing to escape to the garage and his own project.

"Well, we're *not*," Marina said emphatically, "until next year," she added. She could see by the set of his shoulders that he wasn't happy, but she pressed on anyway out of habit. It was the way she got things done.

"I've got the whole weekend off, so we'll start at the top of Mr. Holmgren's list—the gutters."

Paris was astonished, "He said the header was the most important thing."

"Everything Mr. Holmgren said is important," Marina bristled, "I'm doing things in the most *practical* order."

Paris stiffened and tried not to say what was on his mind.

"What?" she asked, recognizing that he was holding something back. The problem with troublesome inner thoughts is that they tend to escape through our mouths, especially when something important is at stake and we feel cornered.

Paris blurted, "If you want to work on the gutters first, fine! But the header *is* the most important thing," he paused watching her expression turn to stone, and added, "and you know it."

Marina took a deep breath, "I'll get to the header," she said in measured tones that sounded steadier than she felt. She wanted him to back off, but he let his words fly because he couldn't keep them in check any more.

"You can't fix it by yourself, but you won't admit it!" he blurted.

Marina wasn't ready to admit anything, but she didn't want to lose her temper.

"Just work with me here, Paris," she said between clenched teeth. Brushing past him, she pushed open the screen door and went out. He watched her disappear around the side of the house, and then followed her into the yard.

"Heads up!" Marina said, tossing him a pair of work gloves.

Paris caught them and turned away so that she wouldn't see how much it hurt to pull them on over his bruised hands. He glanced up at Janos's balcony. Sure enough, Janos was up there, drinking coffee and sunning himself like Zippo. No sign that he'd found the camera.

"Paris, I'm talking to you!" Marina said sternly.

"What?"

"I need your full attention. This is dirty, dangerous work," she said.

"I'm here, Mom," Paris said earnestly. She gave him a nod, and went up the ladder. As she went about ripping into the rotted wood and yanking down the old gutters, he couldn't help admiring her strength and determination. For the next few hours, he would obey her commands, although at times he showed no more enthusiasm than a condemned prisoner.

Their work gloves protected their hands, but they still managed to get scrapes and splinters on their arms and necks. They worked well together, but their minds went in different directions. Marina was sure that Paris was simply too young to understand all that she was dealing with. Paris tried to forget about the parade; but its energy was everywhere, carried on the air by music and laughter. What made it worse was that all morning and into the afternoon, no one stopped by or said hello. It was as if Marina had hung a huge *Do Not Disturb* sign on the house.

From time to time, Paris looked over at Janos's place. It was hard to say for sure, but it seemed that sometimes Janos was watching them. As soon as Paris caught his eye, though, Janos looked away. Had he found the camera? Should Paris wave hello? *No,* Paris told himself. *Be cool.*

Finally, late in the afternoon, Randi Leonardo came into the yard, and Paris was glad for the interruption.

"I know you guys are busy, but we got pizza, and this one was left over," she said, holding up a large pizza box. Paris grabbed the box eagerly. Marina grabbed it back.

"No thanks, Randi," she said.

"Oh for goodness sakes, Marina," Randi said, giving it back to Paris, "It's pineapple and Canadian bacon. Ish!"

"I *love* that!" Paris said, opening the box and tearing off a piece.

Randi winked at Marina.

"Well, okay. On behalf of my starving son, thank you," Marina conceded.

Paris stuffed the rest of the slice into his mouth and took the box over to the back steps, where he sat down and tore off one more.

"He's a growing kid, Marina," Randi said, "he needs to eat like ten times a day."

Marina smiled somewhat stiffly.

"Yell if you need anything," Randi said kindly.

"I will," Marina said.

"No, you won't," Randi mumbled on her way out.

Marina joined Paris on the back steps and tore off a slice of pizza.

"Tomorrow, we can start putting up the new stuff," she said with her mouth full.

Then, without thinking, she wiped some tomato sauce from his chin. Playfully, Paris grabbed her chin and did the same. And that is pretty much how the combination of hunger, humor and hard work smoothed over the rough patches between them. As evening approached and Marina was winding up her work, Paris looked up at the balcony. Janos was gone, and Paris hoped that he had the camera with him.

CHAPTER TWENTY EIGHT

While Paris stood outside in the fading light of day wondering about Janos and the camera, Janos sat in his lamp lit living room wondering by what miracle the camera had come back to him. He lifted its familiar weight up to his eye and looked through the lens. His father used to call it his *Magic Mirror.*

"It reflects life because it captures the light that touches us," he'd say reverently. He was always in a hurry to develop his photographs. His enthusiasm was infectious. The whole family—aunts, uncles, cousins—loved his pictures. Janos never knew people so crazy about photographing themselves. Tears rose to his eyes, and he put down the camera. It had been a long time since his grief had broken through like this. He pinched the bridge of his nose and pressed his fingertips into the corners of his eyes. It was the incident in the barn, when he saved that boy from the horse. Touching someone in distress after so many years of cultivated aloofness and a kind of self-imposed exile had unnerved him. He had started remembering people and missing them again.

With the recollection of his father's words, he had "heard" Bosnian again. He hadn't realized how much he missed its fluid qualities. His American thinking was a tedious chore by comparison. There was too much punctuation in English, not enough music. His heart carried him to places that his head preferred to avoid. Where he came from, it used to be that no one lived outside of family. One had a place; one was connected always—to the past and the future—by stories and holy days, weddings, and funerals. No one ever imagined that all of those connections, and all of those people could be wiped out in a matter of hours.

He picked up the camera again, and ran his finger along the white edge of the silver pigeon feather that was tied to the neck strap. It was unlikely to be the mark of the red-haired thief who stole the camera. It was too whimsical. Someone else must have intervened, but who would do such a thing for him? He had been so good at remaining a stranger wherever he went.

He tried to remember if he had seen anyone or anything that might give away the identity of his benefactor. The morning had begun ordinarily enough with the usual drone of weekend lawn mowing—an American obsession that he would never understand. But by the time he stepped out on the porch with his coffee, the noise of the lawnmowers were but the tip of the iceberg. Overnight, back yards and driveways had become staging grounds for circus acts and several improbable construction projects—at least one pirate ship and the beginnings of a Chinese dragon.

Next door, however, a different kind of work was underway, characterized by the noise of crumpling and ripping metal. Paris and his mother were pulling down old gutters, and judging from the pile of new gutters, Marina was going to install them with only the help of her son. From what he could hear, she gave instructions as well as any foreman, but he thought it was foolish for a woman to tackle such a big job on her own. Paris looked up at him, but as soon as their eyes met, the boy looked away. *Good*, Janos thought. As far as he was concerned, the sooner the horse and the barn thing were forgotten, the better.

Beyond the Thibideaux yard, Janos could see the man who played golf in his back yard. Today, he looked weak, and his companion seemed to be doing all the putting. Janos admired the men for laughing together for hours even though it was obvious that Death was slowly overtaking one of them. Janos had forgotten that Death is not always brutal and abrupt.

Across the alley, lay the glorified junkyard of the two nosy mechanics. They were busy adding a new fixture to what looked like a tower of toilets. Janos could appreciate the clownish spectacle, but he thought that Pete and Blossum enjoyed their eccentricity a little too much. He would never let them work on his truck.

The one tranquil spot on the block was the garden of the Hmong woman. She tended it daily on her hands and knees. Like him, she was far from her homeland, having been displaced by war. But she had escaped with her family. This morning she sat at a picnic table with a little girl making something out of paper. Like his mother, she was always at ease with the little ones.

"G'morning, Janos!" Max Christensen called from below.

Janos rested his elbows on the porch rail and waved his cup in the direction of the alley, "What's going on?"

Max was pleasantly surprised. He had come to expect very little in the way of conversation from his new tenant.

"It's getting close to the Parade, you know," he spluttered.

"It's a big deal, eh?" Janos offered.

Max squinted up at him, charmed.

"Oh, the biggest," he said proudly, "whole families—two, three generations—come out. It's like . . . a whatchacallit . . ."

"A tradition," Janos filled in.

"Yeah, exactly!" Max exclaimed.

"Oh, Max, leave the man alone!" Solveigh scoffed. From the back door, Mrs. Christenson squinted up at Janos with one hand shading her eyes. Janos felt his face crack into a grin. Max's wife had a sharp, eagle-like countenance that contrasted with Max's apple-cheeked enthusiasm, but her sharpness was a bluff that was belied by her twinkling eyes. In the short time that he had been living there, she had already left him, just outside his door, a number of covered dishes with delicious meatloaf and casseroles that she called "hot dish."

"You like pie, Mr. Kovac? I'm baking pies this morning. I'll save you one," she said.

"I like pie, Mrs. Christenson, but no need . . ."

"Oh, no bother. I'll leave it for you in a tin. God knows, you can't leave any foodstuffs uncovered with that glutton Two-Ton around," she said before disappearing into her kitchen. Suddenly, the door flew open again, and Two-Ton came out with his head hung low and his tail between his legs.

"That dog ate a whole rhubarb pie!" Solveigh complained to Max, "You keep him outside now."

Max turned skeptically to the dog, "Really? A whole pie?"

He bent to wipe the rhubarb goo from the dog's muzzle with his handkerchief, and the two ambled off together. Janos sipped his coffee. It was strong. He liked it black with no sugar, but when he was a baby his first coffee was mostly milk and sugar that his mother let him sip from a tiny spoon. She was on his mind this morning. She used to love parades and pageants, and preparing for festivals. But Janos couldn't forget that everything people are capable of building in a community, they can destroy in minutes. Neighbors can turn on neighbors, and Janos still couldn't see one side of the coin without recalling the other. Balancing on the back legs of his chair, he lifted his face to the warmth of the sun.

His eyes came to rest on something that glinted among the branches of the tree right in front of him. Instantly, he recognized his camera! He leaned precariously over the railing and snatched it, clasping it to his chest. Oddly, a pigeon feather fluttered on the end of a string tied to the neck strap.

Now, hours later, having combed through his recollections of the day, he still had no clue as to who might have returned it to him. And beyond that, there was the mystery of the numbers in the frame count window—it read 36; his father had only shot 27. The camera still held the last roll of film his father had shot, among them the last picture ever taken of Janos with his two sons and baby girl. He had never been able to bring himself to develop it and had been it carrying around all these years, locked in the dark inside the camera.

When we look at photographs, our gaze is drawn to the light, and with human subjects, the light is in the eyes. Until the camera was taken from him, Janos thought he could never bear to see the light captured in eyes that had closed forever. Now, it appeared that someone had added nine images of their own, and it seemed imperative to develop the film right away, if only to separate the intruders from his family.

CHAPTER TWENTY NINE

After the long day of working on the gutters, Marina still had a list of things to do inside the house that night. But by nine o'clock, she began to fade, giving Paris hope that he might be able to sneak out to the garage and work on his project. When she took off her shoes around nine-thirty, she started snoring almost as soon as she sat down. Paris nudged her gently, "Mom, go to bed."

"No," she moaned like a child and buried her face in the soft cushiony chair.

Paris laughed, "We can get started early again tomorrow. You're off, remember?"

He took her hands and helped her to her feet.

"Gee, Paris," she murmured, resting her head on his shoulder. It hurt where she leaned on his sore ear, but he wasn't about to complain.

They climbed the stairs together, and at her bedroom door, she kissed him and put her hand on his chest, "Such a big help, you . . ." she said trailing off.

"G'night, Mom," he said firmly.

From his own room, he listened with mounting impatience to the movements of her bedtime routine. As soon as all was quiet, he slipped out of the house. He had reached that point in the creation of his parade project that required welding to raise it from a heap of scrap metal on the floor to a freestanding, parade-worthy whatever-it-was. For a lot of reasons, especially because his mother would never forgive them, Paris decided not to ask Pete and Blossum for help with the welding. Tonight, he would simply "borrow" Pete's gear. He called it *Operation Juice Cart*.

Outside, the chirpings of crickets and the flickering lights of fireflies had a calming effect on Paris; that is, until he reached the door of Pete and Blossum's shop, over which they had hung a large "Keep Out" sign. He contemplated the various booby traps that could be inside, but there was no turning back now. The door closed behind him and plunged him into a consuming darkness. The pungent odors of the shop—solvents, soaps, fuel, cigars, and coffee—burned his nose. It was hard to tell where his body ended, and the dark began. He felt like one of those sea creatures crawling sightless at the bottom of the deepest darkest depths of the ocean.

He kept his eyes wide open, anyway, and gradually the hulking shape of Pete's workbench emerged in shades of gray from the black landscape. He turned on his flashlight. There was a tarp thrown over the workbench. He lifted it, and there underneath was the "Juice Cart," the rolling heap of batteries, wires and clamps mounted on the frame of a child's wagon. Paris moved quickly to gather up the rest of the welding gear and piled it on the cart.

Pulling the creaking and groaning cart toward the door, he barely breathed. Suddenly, he knew that *he was not alone*. He turned off the flashlight and went into a crouch behind the Juice Cart. All of a sudden something jumped on to the cart, and Paris almost yelped. A pair of gleaming eyes peered down at him.

"Zippo!" Paris gasped, as the cat vanished. He might have been an apparition but for the nails or screws that jingled to the floor like loose change.

It was slow going getting the Juice Cart out of the shop and across the alley. It squealed like a pig for lack of oil. By the time he reached the door of his own garage, Paris should have been exhausted, but he was gripped by excitement and surprising energy. Inside a pile of discarded scrap metal, wood, and pieces of plastic waited for him. Out here, Paris was just a boy with a fantastic idea, but once he stepped into the workspace he would be an artist with fire in his hands.

In another part of that same night, Janos Kovac, the Bosnian, sat at his kitchen table, holding the envelope of photographs. He thought about blunting his emotions with alcohol, but then he might miss something. He didn't want to miss anything now. He took a deep breath and removed pictures from the package. The first picture was of a boy, a blurry, smiling self-portrait that Janos recognized instantly: Paris.

He knew now that Paris must have taken the camera away from the thief at considerable risk. The second and third photographs were of Marina. She was asleep on the couch in her living room, and although he thought she looked lovely, he also felt like he was eavesdropping. He dropped all of the photos on the table, and fanned them out like a deck of cards—Bosnian people next to Powderhorn people and the Thibideaux family mixed up with the Kovac clan.

He set aside Marina and Paris. Then with trembling hands, he dealt out the rest like a game of Solitaire. They were from his brother's wedding. Everyone had been there. Janos was in most of the pictures hugging, kissing, posing with babies and old people, dancing with his wife and his mother, and standing proudly with his children. Too proudly, it seemed now. Looking at these images now was painful, but it was a beautiful kind of pain to see everyone again. One could almost believe they were still living. There was no sign above Janos's head indicating that he alone would survive.

His father's pictures told the story of that day so well that even strangers could grasp that love and humor and two great traditions were alive among these people, Christian and Muslim. On such a joyous day, no one could have foreseen how quickly history could swallow generations, and deposit Janos half a world away, all alone, peering through these little windows into that world where he was still dancing with his wife and children, still toasting the happy couple. Next door in the garage, Paris suited up and prepared to create personal lightning.

CHAPTER THIRTY

Paris pulled the welder's helmet down onto his head and slipped his hands into the big leather gloves. Like Pete, he wore a jacket to protect himself from burns. When he flipped down the mask and peered through its window, he felt like a knight suited up for battle. And in a way, he was. War and welding are both dangerous work. The danger in welding is not only the heat and the sparks, but also the ultra violet light and toxic chemicals generated by the process. The kind of welding that Pete had taught him was arc or "stick" welding. It's a slow process. The electrical current (a lot of it) flows from the source, in this case the Juice Cart, to the "stick" or wand. Paris prepared to "strike an arc" by scratching the electrode wand against the first piece of metal. Once he had the arc of electricity, he pulled back the wand just enough to keep the arc going.

He could feel the crackle and spark of the electricity when he applied it to the metal. DZZZZZT! DZZZZT! The raw electricity pulled him along. It almost felt like dancing. Pete had said, "Each welder has his own style of weaving with the welds. I want you to watch me, but when it's your turn, forget everything and let your own style come through."

Piece by piece, Paris forced rusty rebar, scrap iron and sheet metal into the third dimension. The flat outline he had laid out on the floor began to stand up on its own. Reflected in the window of the mask, the cascade of sparks looked like giant fireflies clinging to a creature that came from pure light and heat. Outside, the stars in the night sky were sharp and brilliant, and from the alley, the garage pulsed with a bluish white glow as Paris's arc lit up the loft windows and spilled into the alley.

Maybe ancient Gods worked the way Paris worked that night, using borrowed fire to make their visions into something alive and free. Paris worked through the night and into the predawn hours, and as he did, he learned to move with his wand in a way that was sweeping and spontaneous, but also steady and smooth. He had found his "style" and was transforming the whispers of his imagination into something grand and untamed. When he began he thought he was building a scrap metal skeleton that he would fill out later with chicken wire and *papier mache*—like a school project, only bigger. Add a dab of paint, a few feathers, a wheeled platform—and roll it down the parade route. But the form taking shape in front of him now, in the hybrid light of sparks and incandescence, had become much more than the bare bones of something else.

At last, Paris withdrew the arc and shut down the Juice Cart. He stepped away and lifted the mask from his face. He took off the helmet and gloves, and found that he was dripping with perspiration. Then, he took a good long hard look at his hands. Over the past couple of days, they had done battle with a giant horse and a spiteful bully. They were bashed and aching, but they had made *that* which now stood before him, its neck proudly arched, its feet planted firmly, looking back at him. It almost breathed. If he squinted just so, it looked as though it might just walk for him.

When he emerged from the garage, clouds covered the stars. He had oiled the wheels on the Juice Cart so it was quiet, but every crunch and crackle of gravel under the wagon wheels made him flinch. Just as he reached Pete and Blossum's garage, a car turned into the alley and turned off its headlights. Paris dove headlong into some tall weeds and yanked the cart after him. As the car rolled closer, Paris recognized it. Felix Ermler turned into the Thibideaux driveway and parked. He got out and stood staring at the house. Then, he opened the gate and went into the yard, disappearing from view behind the garage. Paris scurried out of the weeds to a better vantage point from Dan's side of the alley. Ermler was looking over the new gutters Marina had stacked in the yard. At last he got back into his car. The lighted dial of his cell phone bathed his face in a ghoulish green glow until he snapped it shut and drove toward the other end of the alley. He didn't turn his headlights back on until he was in the street. What the heck was that all about? It couldn't be good, Paris thought, to have your landlord prowling around in the middle of the night.

The rest of Operation Juice Cart went without a hitch, and he was home and in bed as the night sky began to brighten. But he lay awake for a long time. Just as he was finally beginning to doze off, he was seized by a horrifying convergence of terrors. Maybe, it was a dream, but whatever it was, it left behind the disturbing notion that Ermler and Billy were cut from the same cloth. Felix was probably as furious about the possibility of losing the house to Marina, as Billy was about losing the camera to Paris. Ermler was a just another street bully, but with a car and an office.

CHAPTER THIRTY ONE

With the sound of a screen door slamming, Marina trotted down the steps, across the yard and out into the alley. It had been a very productive weekend. They had spent Saturday ripping down the old gutters and Sunday putting up the new. Now, she was off to her day job bright and early Monday morning. From his balcony, Janos watched as she walked briskly toward the bus stop on Lake Street. He didn't take much notice of women generally, but she was hard to ignore. He had to admit that he admired her because, despite her stubbornness, she was a woman of phenomenal energy—but that was none of his business, he told himself. He turned his attention to a small leather bundle that he had carried with him from Bosnia. It contained his pocketknife, a small block of wood, a sharpening stone and a small tin of mineral oil. He untied the lacings and unrolled it, releasing the familiar aromas of basswood and oiled leather. It felt good to bring the knife's sharp edge to bear on the wood, which gave off a faint scent of honey. It was more like peeling than cutting, revealing the next layer, opening up to possibilities revealed in the grain. He was at peace with the wood.

Normally, Janos would have been at work by now, but he had the morning off because of a late shipment of shingles that wouldn't be delivered to the work site until noon, at the earliest. People and cars came and went through the alley, but Janos was an expert at minding his own business. He had always found it easy to be alone in public, but he had no idea that eventually it would become his whole way of life.

A sleek black Mercedes with tinted windows cruised into the alley and stopped just short of the Thibideaux house. For a moment, before the driver rolled down his window, Janos had a brief notion that armed men in black shirts might get out and take someone away. That was a throwback to the Old World, but this was America, and in this car was just one man. Neither he nor his car was *of* this neighborhood, Janos observed. Children playing in the alley ran away from the car, but one boy, came right up to it. Of course, it was *the* boy, the red-haired camera thief.

Janos continued to carve, but his attention was effectively divided between the sweet-smelling wood shavings raised by his knife and the two suspicious characters in the alley that, Janos was certain, were up to no good. The man passed something to the boy as if to confirm Janos's instincts that he was looking at people doing business. Suddenly, the window rolled up. The man and the boy went off in opposite directions. Janos did not get a good look at the driver, but he memorized the car. He was paying attention—although to all appearances he was only carving a block of wood.

CHAPTER THIRTY TWO

Wrrrrrrrrt! WRT! It was the sound of a bad tool being used badly. Paris had convinced Marina to let him have the job of attaching new wooden spindles to the back porch rail, and he was working, or rather fumbling, with an ancient electric drill. The drill was heavy and hard to steady, so instead of the drill bit spinning down into a spindle, the spindle was spinning like a propeller on the end of the drill bit. Paris did not linger in frustration long. He gave it one long *Wrrrrrrrrrrrrrrrt!* until it flew over the rail and skittered across the pavement below. Jumping from the steps to retrieve it, Paris found himself face to face with Janos.

"This drill makes a terrible noise," Janos said drily, "it is older than me."

Paris opened his mouth, but no words came out.

Janos picked up the spindle and examined it, "If you make a jig, is much easier. I show you."

He grabbed a few blocks of wood and a hammer, struck some pencil marks, and hammered the blocks in place.

"You put each spindle in here and place drill in line with this mark. Then, use post to guide. Each hole will be always the same."

Janos took his own cordless drill from its holster and demonstrated, "See? Is easy."

He offered Paris his drill, "You try," he said.

Paris looked over his shoulder toward the house.

"I insist," Janos added.

In Paris's hand, the drill made a smooth and regular mechanical sound much like a cat's purr and made a perfect hole in the spindle. Janos handed him another spindle. Paris drilled another perfect hole. They continued working together in silence, and Paris became completely absorbed in the rhythm and ease of it.

"And thanks for my camera," Janos said abruptly.

Paris stopped drilling and smiled to himself.

"Just bring back my drill when you're done," Janos said and turned to leave.

"Paris, who are you talking to?" Marina asked, opening the screen door.

Paris jumped to attention, "This is Janos from next door. He's building the new stables at the park," and to Janos he quickly added, "and this is my Mom."

Marina's eyes had fixed on the bright yellow cordless drill in Paris's hand.

Janos explained, "He had a very old drill, so I lend him mine."

Marina nodded, at a loss for words.

"He handles it well, if that's okay with you," he added, remembering that mothers like to be consulted.

Paris looked up at Janos standing tall and strong in his black T-shirt and work jeans. He looked like he could fix anything. How could she not be impressed?

"Nice to meet you, Mrs. . . um," Janos hesitated, looking to Paris.

"Thibideaux," Paris said.

"Marina," she said, extending her right hand. Her left hand flew up to brush back some hair that had fallen over her eyes. Janos clasped her hand and said, "Janos Kovac."

Paris had no clear idea what he wanted to happen next, but he was sure that if he left things up to the grown-ups, they would blow it. So he made like a doorman at a great hotel and opened the back door.

"Wanna come in and see what we're doing?"

The grown-ups froze.

"Come on," he prodded, waving Janos toward the door.

"After you, Mrs. Thibideaux," Janos said awkwardly.

Marina and Janos stopped just inside the kitchen door as though their shoes were glued to the floor. Paris pushed past them.

"Mom's doing a great job," he said.

"I can see that," Janos said.

Marina's jaw relaxed into a tentative smile. Paris led the way to the living room.

"It's a work site," Marina said, "that's why it's such a mess."

Janos saw past the construction clutter to the beautifully refinished floors and the expert blend of new and old woods in the picture molding and doorframes, and he said so.

"Thank you," Marina said modestly.

Then he spotted the header and the makeshift brace Marina had built. Suddenly, as if on cue, the crude wooden support groaned ominously. Marina grabbed a hammer and a handful of nails from the coffee table. Janos picked up another and joined in.

"Brace it here on diagonal," Janos said, lining up a two-by-four.

"I know where to brace it," Marina said testily. When Janos wasn't looking, she turned to Paris and gave him an "I'll deal with you later" look.

Janos sensed that she didn't like being told what to do in her own house, but he was more worried about the collapse of the brace. Paris, on the other hand, was enjoying watching them work together in spite of his mother's threatening looks. When they finished reinforcing the brace, both Janos and Marina stepped back and said, "Good" at the same time.

Good for grown-ups, Paris thought.

Janos looked around uncomfortably, like he was planning an escape. Paris grabbed the little black book of Marina's notes and sketches and showed it to Janos.

"These are the plans my Mom makes," Paris said proudly, holding it open and turning the pages.

"This is very good," Janos said sincerely.

"Yeah, she's a good artist," Paris said, turning pages excitedly for Janos.

"Okay, that's enough!" Marina exclaimed, snatching it away and hugging it protectively, "They're just scribbles."

"You do *all* construction?" Janos asked.

"Pretty much," Marina answered modestly, "*we* did," she added, pointing from Paris to herself.

"Is good," Janos nodded approvingly.

A hint of a smile played at the corners of Marina's mouth. It had been a long time since she had allowed a man to visit. They tended to fall into acting like "the big man" and treating her like the "little woman," and she had no patience for that. Janos *seemed* different, but she didn't trust her first impressions. Paris thought she was about to end the conversation, but she surprised him.

"I have to redo the casements on the dining room window," she said dropping to her knees by the window to show him where.

"I see, yes," Janos said, joining her. In the late afternoon light, Paris thought he looked younger, although it was clear from the gray in his hair and whiskers, that he was a good bit older than Marina. Nevertheless, Paris liked seeing them together inspecting the window frame and talking easily about water damage and sill replacement. Then they ran out of things to say. Janos cleared his throat, and they both looked lost.

"I think is time I should go now," Janos said politely.

"Come take a look at the kitchen," Paris insisted, saying the first words that popped into his head.

"Paris!" Marina blushed, "the man says he has to go."

But Paris was already hauling Janos into the kitchen.

"What do you think?" he asked boldly, "Not bad, huh?"

"Paris, stop it," Marina said.

"No," Janos said, addressing Marina, "you are fine craftsman, -*woman*, I mean," he said appreciatively, "how much longer you think this will take?"

"I have a month," she said.

Janos grinned, "You keep little contractors hiding around here?"

"No, no contractors," Marina said stiffly.

For Paris, it was like watching a train wreck in slow motion.

"You joking?" Janos laughed nervously.

"I don't joke about my house," Marina bristled.

Paris felt his spirit sinking with every word Marina said.

"I don't own the house yet," she continued, "The owner has given me thirty days to get a loan and buy it or get out. He's got someone else who's ready to buy it outright."

Why does she have to blab to him about our troubles? Paris fumed helplessly.

"After all the work you've done," Janos asked, "he can do this?"

"Yes, he can," Marina said simply, "it's part of the contract I signed."

"But even my crew couldn't do this job in thirty days," Janos said, shaking his head.

"Well, I'm sure you know your crew," Marina's back had stiffened to match her voice, "but you have no idea what I am capable of."

"Maybe not, but I'm a sensible man," Janos said.

"And that makes all the difference, eh, being a man?

"No, being *sensible*. . ." Janos retorted.

"When I finish," Marina cut him off, "I can borrow money from the bank and pay him what the contract calls for."

"Mom! Nobody wants to hear . . ." Paris tried to intervene.

"You are very busy, I go now," Janos said with strained politeness.

121

Marina stood silently with her arms folded across her chest. Janos practically dashed to the back door. Paris let him pass, and then moved to follow him.

"Oh, no you don't!" Marina grabbed his arm and spun him around, "Since when do you bring strangers into our house?"

"He was invited—by me! It's my house, too."

"I don't need his help," Marina snapped.

"You don't know how to fix the header!" Paris shot back.

Marina slammed her fist on the table, "I don't need that man coming in here telling me what to do!"

"Then, you don't need me, either!" Paris said shoving the screen door open and slamming it with such force that it closed with a loud clap of wood on wood.

CHAPTER THIRTY THREE

Anger swept over Paris. He didn't know exactly what he had been hoping for, but it certainly wasn't this—his mother being all prickly and proud, and Janos literally running away. Paris could see that he was already in his truck, about to drive away. The drill caught his eye, lying on the top step among the scattered spindles. Its sunny yellow plastic trim taunted him. It had seemed to be the answer to a prayer, the promise of good will and a helping hand for his mother, who desperately needed help, but was too stubborn to admit it. It was clear now that the drill was nothing more than a tool borrowed from a neighbor. He grabbed the drill and ran blindly with it into the alley.

"Keep it!" he would say to Janos.

But the truck was already gone.

WHAM! The ground came up and hit Paris in the face like a slamming door. He was thrown like a sack of rubbish against the alley side of the garage. Dust went up his nose and made him choke, and the taste of dirt filled his mouth. The next thing he knew, he was on his back, and something like a boulder dropped on to his chest. The drill had been ripped from his hand.

Billy pressed one knee heavily into Paris's chest, pinning him to the ground. He held the drill an inch from Paris's nose. Paris needed to cough, but he was paralyzed. Billy menaced every inch of Paris's face with the deadly spinning bit. Right eye. Left eye. Right cheek. Chin. Paris's face contorted into a mask of fear. Billy loomed over him, brandishing the drill. It was everywhere, threatening to rip into his skin and bore through his skull, and he couldn't fight back. The more Paris shrank from the hot air gusting from the drill's exhaust, the more the gravel dug cruelly into the back of his head.

"Open your eyes, Paris," Billy commanded, "I want you to see this."

Paris blinked helplessly and took in the face of his tormentor, who was holding the drill high above his head.

"Here comes the big one!"

Paris screamed as Billy made a wild pass downward across his face. A bone-rattling clatter and vibration shook Paris so that he thought the drill was boring into his forehead. But it was actually embedded in the wooden siding of the garage just inches above Paris's head. Billy swore and tugged at it, but the drill was stuck. Paris bucked and squirmed free.

On unsteady legs, he ran into Dan's yard thrashing like a drowning man. Tommy had been sitting on the steps, but he stood when he saw Paris. Dan was on the green, leaning against his walker, calculating his next putt. A plastic oxygen tube wound like a snake around his head, through the legs of his walker, and connected to a green oxygen tank on wheels. Paris sprinted past Dan and collapsed at Tommy's feet. Billy was only a few steps behind him, bellowing and waving the cordless drill in the air, but he tripped over Dan's plastic tubing and took the walker and the oxygen tank with him to the ground.

"GEEZ!" Dan cried, as his head snapped back, and he fell to his knees, choking.

"Hold on, Dan!" Tommy yelled as he picked Billy up by his collar.

"Damn!" Dan retorted as he lay down on the ground, coughing and gasping for air. Billy pulled the trigger on the drill, and tried to turn it on Tommy. But Tommy snatched it out of Billy's hand like a toy and gave his collar an extra twist.

"Ow! Let go, you crazy Indian!" Billy screamed as Tommy marched him on tiptoes out into the alley.

"You vex me, Bill," Tommy said, releasing the boy, "I'd keep goin' *that* way, if I was you," he added indicating a great distance with a broad sweep of his arm. Billy backed away, muttering. Tommy froze and Billy, mistaking this for weakness, repeated his insults out loud while waving his middle fingers in Tommy's face. Tommy sprang forward and uttered a blood-curdling cry. Billy turned and ran for his life.

Tommy went to Dan, who was on the ground, kicking the heck out of the walker and trying to untangle himself from the oxygen tubing.

"Stop it, Dan," Tommy said, "you're gonna hurt yourself!"

"This is what's gonna kill me!" Dan declared angrily, ripping the plastic tubing from his face, "all this . . . this . . . *crap*!"

"Are you done?" Tommy asked, stopping him from ripping at the tubing.

"Yeah, I'm done," Dan said, wilting.

As Tommy untangled the tubing, and righted the oxygen tank and the walker, Dan looked up at him and asked, "Did you make Billy cry?"

"No," Tommy grinned, "I made him *run*."

"Heh, heh," Dan laughed as Tommy helped him up and eased him to the edge of the porch next to Paris.

"Don't let him go nowhere," Tommy said to Paris.

"Leave me alone, will ya?" Dan barked.

"Are you gonna behave, or do I have to call Aunt Helen?" Tommy asked, "you want the oxygen?"

"Gimme a minute," Dan said, coughing into a crumpled hanky and wiping his mouth.

"I'd like to have a talk with my buddy here," he said, indicating Paris.

Tommy eyed them skeptically, picked up his putter, and moved to the green.

"Pretend I'm not here."

"Not a problem," Dan said cheekily.

Dan and Paris looked like two weary soldiers after a battle. Both faces were flushed from exertion. Paris's chest was still heaving, and he was beginning to feel a pounding headache.

"So, buddy, here we are," said Dan, "you look pretty rough. Try to breathe."

Dan lit a cigarette and drew in the first smoke as if it were a point-of-honor to enjoy the worst possible thing he could do to his health.

"Take it from a sick man, breathing is the key."

Paris wiped his eyes and left streaks of mud on his cheeks and eyelids. He pulled up the bottom of his T-shirt and covered his face, pretending to wipe it, but Dan knew he was hiding. He blew smoke rings and pretended not to notice. After a moment, he leaned close and almost whispered, "Tell me what happened."

Paris sighed, and the words came haltingly, "Billy stole a camera . . . from this guy Janos," he began, "and so . . . I took it, and I, uh . . . gave it back to Janos."

Dan cleared his throat, "He came after you, huh?"

Paris nodded clamping his trembling hands between his knees.

"So, what's the problem? You gave back the loot that he stole," Dan said, leaning back on his elbows, "sounds like you did the right thing."

"I thought so," Paris said.

"What did you expect? You knew it was *dangerous*," Dan started to cough, and although he kept trying to speak, he couldn't catch his breath.

". . . might have been safer . . . mind your own business," he wheezed.

"You don't have to . . ." Paris broke in, but Dan fixed him with a look that made him hush.

"Listen to me," Dan said sternly, "You're a . . . a finder and a fixer . . . that's your nature."

"What about Billy?" Paris asked indignantly.

"It's *your* nature that's important here. Are you gonna be true to yourself or what?" Dan replied, yanking the tail of his shirt up to cover his mouth. When it came away, there was blood on it.

"Shit," he muttered.

"Dan," Paris said, his eyes widening.

"Hand me that beer over there, will ya?" Dan said, tucking in his shirt.

Paris gave him the open can. Dan swirled it around and held it out to Paris.

"You see any cigarette butts in there?" he laughed, "sometimes . . . I forget."

They both laughed. Dan gulped down the beer.

"Okay, listen up," Dan said softly, "come closer. I can't do this twice." Paris leaned in.

"You are the most resourceful boy I ever met. Paris . . . Don't smile! This is not flattery."

He paused, fighting the urge to cough, and began again.

"I mean, when you see something wrong or broken, you don't leave it alone. You do somethin' about it. Don't deny it. I know you . . . important thing is: This . . . not child's play. It's work!"

"Take it easy, will ya, Dan?" Tommy said, "you're wearing yourself out."

Dan waved him off, "Trouble is you made a correction in Billy's column this time. Now, he wants to scare you so you won't ever do it again."

He pulled long and hard on his cigarette, "You see how that works?"

Paris mulled it over, "I guess."

"You *guess*?" Dan was taken aback, "You can't let a bully scare you out of being who you are, who you were meant to be."

"But I did take the camera," Paris said.

"This is not about a *camera*. This is about a bully trying to break you! BE yourself, Paris, no matter what." Dan said, his voice trailing off at the end. His eyes fluttered, and he dropped his cigarette. A smile spread across his face, and at the same time his body seemed to collapse like a balloon with a slow leak. He came to rest against Paris's shoulder, and Paris put an arm around him. He had become so frail that Paris thought a pile of leaves would have more resistance to a strong wind. Tommy came and sat down on the other side and got Dan to take some oxygen.

Dan sighed, "You guys are great."

Paris looked at Tommy. Dan removed the tubing from his nose and spoke very softly, "Paris, are you listening 'cause I don't have much wind."

"I'm listening," Paris assured him.

"People get scared—and they give up on themselves. A bully can do that to you."

Paris couldn't hide his tears now, but Dan didn't seem to mind. He shook his head and continued in a voice that was low but steady, "Billy's gonna keep trying to scare you, and you *should* be scared of him. He's mean and he's strong. But having a bully around is not the end of the world. It just means you have to be a little quicker and a little smarter. Ask yourself: are you gonna be the one and only Paris Thibideaux or some frightened little soul with the same name?"

"Come on, Dan," Tommy said, "You're taking more oxygen now."

Dan nodded, and Tommy helped him on to the sofa. Paris wiped his eyes. Every word Dan said had weighed on his heart like a stone. They sounded like last words, somehow, and he wasn't ready to hear last words from Dan. Paris lifted the oxygen tank to the porch. Dan leaned back and promptly fell asleep. They arranged a light quilt over him, and then sat quietly together on the steps. Every once in a while Tommy cleared his throat and looked away.

CHAPTER THIRTY FOUR

The Paradise Bakery got some new customers, and Marina got a new delivery route. She had to put in extra hours learning it. As a result, Paris had a whole afternoon and evening to be alone in his workshop. He didn't have to think about Billy or the house or his mother, who for once hadn't left him a list of things to get done. All he had to do was build. He mixed up a big batch of *papier mache*, a magical substance he had learned to make in elementary school and started right away placing the paste-soaked strips of newsprint carefully over the sculpted chicken wire. Working his way from the back to the front, Paris placed the strips and smoothed them.

He had never made anything so big, and it wasn't easy. He would lay on the layers of *papier mache* and peel them off again and again trying to get it just right. Eventually, fatigue forced him to close his heavy eyes, and it felt so good that he just went on working that way. Blindly, he smoothed and molded the wet paper, and that was how he found the final shape. It came to him through his fingers.

When he realized that he was running low on newsprint, he chose some areas to leave uncovered, planning to come back to them later, but when he sat down a little distance from his work, he was glad that he was almost out of newsprint. Seeing the "bones" exposed—ribs, legs, neck, and the structure of the hooves—gave it a certain nobility and primitive beauty. This was no merry-go-round horse.

Paris felt very proud and very, very tired. It took him a while to clean up. He didn't want to leave his magnificent horse surrounded by trash and clutter. He even swept the floor to cut down on the dust that was always circulating in the air. It was dark when he finished and went back to the house, climbed the stairs, and tried to sleep. He had every intention of washing up and getting all the bits of paste and *papier mache* out of his hair and off of his skin, but a pleasant dreaminess took over as he climbed into bed. He pulled the kindly darkness around him along with the top sheet and fell into a deep sleep. Nothing but blue and clear and peace as far as his dreamy state would allow.

But in the misty distance, a pulsing red beacon appeared. He awakened with a jolt to flashing red lights bouncing around his room. His first thought was "Fire!" But this light was different, and he'd seen it before. It came with voices and car doors opening and closing outside in the street. He ran to the window. His heart sank as he recognized the pulsing glow—an ambulance in front of Dan's house, its red lights swirling in the night. Dan was on a stretcher in the middle of the front yard. He was holding an unlit cigarette between his teeth. Paris smiled appreciatively for his friend, the clown. But his heart went out to Helen. She stood alongside Dan, and every now and then she brushed away the hair from Dan's forehead the way moms do for their little boys. The ambulance driver came around and spoke to Dan.

"Now, eh?" Dan said, staring up at the night sky, "how about never? Never would be good for me!" His dry laugh turned to a wheeze and then a cough.

"Oh, Danny, be quiet now," Helen scolded, taking away the cigarette.

The medic gave him oxygen as Helen stood by looking lost. Her hair had been loosely pinned, and it fell out around her shoulders almost to her waist. Paris had never seen it unpinned before. Dan took out the oxygen tubes and reached for her, "C'm 'ere, Ma, it's okay," he said smoothing his mother's hair and patting her back gently. She let out a stifled cry. Then, she replaced the tubing so that her son could breathe more easily.

Dan's face was turned toward Paris now, and he could tell from the movements of Dan's chest that it was hard for him to breathe, even with the oxygen. Suddenly, he had the most extraordinary feeling that Dan knew he was there. The moment stretched out like a thin rubber band, and finally it snapped! The medical team went into high gear. Everything became quick and efficient as they lifted Dan into the ambulance. Helen followed, the doors closed, and the ambulance drove away. No sirens. Just the rhythm of the ambulance lights. Pulse—and pulse—and pulse. Wherever the light was going, Dan's heart was going with it.

Paris backed away from the window and wandered into his mother's empty room. Her dresser was cluttered with stuff, including a pile of clean laundry. He lay down on her bed, which had a harder mattress than his. He used to love to jump on it when he was little. That was a different time, he thought, when his mother was simply everything to him. Was it the same for Dan and his mother? Had he just watched Helen and Dan coming to the end of their time together?

He turned his face to the pillow and pulled it up around his ears. It helped him stifle the impulse to cry, and he thought it was better this way. He had heard his mother do it. Now, he understood. After a while he fell asleep breathing in the faint scent of Marina's hair that clung to the pillowcase.

CHAPTER THIRTY FIVE

It wasn't until the day before Dan's funeral that Paris went back to the barn. The mare greeted him with a quick nuzzle and immediately started looking for treats. Paris put his arms around her neck and leaned lightly against her shoulder.

"My friend died," he said, reaching up to touch her chin. It was soft like a ripe peach. She nuzzled his shirt pocket for treats.

"He was sick for a long time," Paris went on, "I used to only see him in his back yard. But now I think I see him all over the place. Out of the corner of my eye, like."

The horse nibbled at his shirt expectantly.

"Tomorrow is his funeral," he said. He pressed his forehead against the warmth of her neck, "I've never been to a funeral."

The horse pressed her nose against his chest forcefully enough to make him take a step back.

"Okay, okay!" Paris said, digging into his back pants pocket for a carrot, "Here."

He listened to the hollow crunching sound of her teeth grinding it to bits and wished she were a better listener. The mare shifted a little the way horses do, and twitched the flies off her hindquarters.

She lowered her head, and he pressed his cheek to hers, "Thanks," he whispered. There was nothing else to say.

He slipped out of the barn and merged into the late afternoon traffic of the park. The hustle of people and trucks around the construction site brightened his mood. Suddenly, Janos came into view, standing several feet in the air, straddling two framed walls. He was confident and at ease with himself in a way that Paris had never seen. It was quite a contrast from the last time he had seen Janos, when he had awkwardly toured the house with Marina. It seemed ages ago, but it had been only a few days. Ever since Dan died, time had become peculiar, slippery, and impossible to pin down.

Paris stood at the back of a group of workers and listened carefully with them to Janos's instructions. He moved about over their heads with some grace in spite of the bulk of his tool belt and the precarious footing. It was obvious that Janos had no fear of heights.

"I need the big wrench, Sam," Janos said, and a man stepped forward and tossed it to him. Janos snatched it out of the air and went back to work. He had not seen Paris yet, but Sam had.

"You need to stay behind the fence, son," Sam said, indicating an orange snow fence, "get back, now. We're busy here, and it's not safe to be this close."

Paris did as he was told, but even at a distance he enjoyed watching Janos. The quiet, moody, unpredictable man was at ease here, and clearly the workers respected him. They were in the process of placing an enormous beam for the new equestrian arena. Raised by a hoist, it had reached the right height now, and Janos guided it into place. Paris watched intently and couldn't help thinking about the header in his own house. Whatever frustration he had felt over the way Janos and Marina had behaved the day they met, seemed irrelevant now. His mother needed an expert to help her with the header. He knew the solution to this problem, and he was completely absorbed in the question of how to bring it about, when someone clamped a hand on his shoulder.

"You need to go, kid," Sam said, "now."

Roused from deep thought, Paris looked puzzled, "Why? I didn't do anything."

"This is a construction site, and we don't have to time to worry where you are every minute," Sam said.

"Okay," Paris said, clearly disappointed.

As Sam turned to go, Paris tugged at his shirtsleeve, "Wait! Could you do me a favor and ask Janos if he could come by on Saturday and give me a hand?"

"What?" Sam asked impatiently.

"Tell him it's Paris's house. He's our neighbor. He knows."

"Go on, get outta here, kid, I'm busy," Sam said, walking away at a brisk pace.

"Just ask him, okay? It's important!" Paris entreated.

"Yeah, sure," Sam said without turning around.

Reluctantly, Paris left the park. When he reached the corner of his street, there were several cars and a couple of motorcycles in front of Dan's house. Tommy was with a group gathered on the front lawn— older people. Guys with long hair and bandannas tied around their heads, some in business suits, and a few men and women wearing military uniforms. Tommy had said that a lot of friends were coming from all over for the funeral, and there were relatives staying with Helen so she wouldn't be alone.

Paris didn't want to be around the crowd, and decided to go up the alley. Helen was sitting alone on her back porch. There were buckets of flowers all around, and their bright green leaves and colorful blossoms seemed out of place. She looked down at a bundle lying in her lap. It was wrapped in brown paper, the tattered ends fluttering slightly in the breeze. She seemed to be wilting like some of the flowers, and Paris wished he could do something for her. He stopped outside her gate, thinking that she looked so alone even though her house was overflowing with people.

"Paris," she said waving, "hello."

"Hi, Mrs. Torvilson," he replied.

"I haven't seen you," she said.

Paris wasn't sure if that was an invitation.

"Come in, come in," Helen said warmly, patting the spot next to her on the sofa.

"Danny's with God, now," she said when he was seated. Paris didn't know what to say. Helen smoothed the crinkled brown paper on her lap and fussed with the yellowed string holding the package together.

"You want to look at this with me?"

"What is it?" Paris asked politely.

Carefully, she pulled open the paper. On top there were some old photos of Dan as a boy playing in Powderhorn Park. It looked like there was a family picnic going on in the background. She ran her finger over a hank of blonde hair wrapped in cellophane.

"From Danny's first haircut . . . Can you believe how blonde it is?" Helen laughed. She opened the packet and ran her finger over the yellow strands.

"When was this?" Paris asked, picking up a photograph of Dan in a tuxedo with his arm around a very pretty girl. She had flowers around her wrist, and her blonde hair was piled high up on her head.

Helen sighed, "Oh, that was Danny's girlfriend. She was the love of his life."

"Where is she?" Paris wondered aloud.

"Well, I don't know. When Danny went into the Marines and off to Vietnam, she married someone else."

"Oh," Paris said, still staring at the picture. Dan's soul was in his eyes and in his smile in spite of all the years since that picture. Kind eyes. And a good soul. Paris began to feel heat rising behind his eyes. He was afraid he would cry, and he didn't want to do that in front of Helen.

Just then, Helen handed him another picture, and Paris laughed out loud.

"Is this Tommy?"

"And Danny," Helen beamed.

It was a snapshot of the two of them when they were about Paris's age, hanging upside down from a branch of the big tree with the bird feeder. Helen picked up another picture of them in their Marine uniforms. With crew cuts, they looked handsome and invincible. Paris wished he had grown up with this other Dan and other Tommy. Suddenly, Helen dumped an envelope full of medals and ribbons into her lap.

"They said Danny was a great leader," she said, "and that a lot of boys would not have come home if it wasn't for Danny."

She looked away for a moment, and then taking up one of the medals, she turned it over in her hand, "Ya! I think Danny would like for you to have this."

She pinned a ribbon with a star hanging from it to Paris's shirt.

"They give this to him for his bravery. He was a Marine, you know," she said.

"Yeah," Paris said.

She put her arm around his shoulders, and they looked through the rest of the photographs and medals in silence. Paris was so absorbed that he didn't hear his own name being called until Marina raised her voice, "Paris!"

He was startled to see his mother standing at Helen's gate.

"Hi, Helen, how are you?" Marina said, "I'm so sorry."

"Come in, dear. Paris is keeping me company," Helen said warmly.

"Well, it's supper time, Paris," Marina said not moving.

"Come in for a minute, Mom," Paris said, "We're looking at some of Dan's pictures and stuff."

Reluctantly, Marina came into the yard. She stood at the bottom of the porch steps.

"Helen," she said hesitating before going on, "there's a double shift at work, and I need to take it. I'm really sorry, but we can't make it to the funeral tomorrow. Is there anything I can do for you?"

"Oh no," Helen said, rising, "that's all right, Marina, but Paris can ride with me if that's all right with you, and if he wants to, that is."

She looked at Paris who was staring at his mother.

"I want to go, Mom," he said flatly.

"All right," Marina said tentatively, "but you've never been to a funeral before."

"I have to go. It's Dan," Paris said.

"Okay," Marina said, "Of course."

Then, she came up on to the porch and hugged Helen who, being taller, rested her cheek on top of Marina's head.

"Where did you get that?" Marina asked, touching the medal on Paris's chest.

"It was Dan's," Paris said, "it's an honor."

Marina looked to Helen, "Is that okay, Helen?"

"Danny would want Paris to keep it for him," Helen said firmly.

At home, Paris and his mother ate dinner in silence. Finally, Marina put her fork down and looked him in the eye, "All right, Paris, let's have it. What's on your mind?"

"I can't believe you're not going to Dan's funeral," he said.

She looked pained, "It's complicated. . ."

"All you care about is work and this house," he said, "it's not complicated."

"That's not fair, Paris. I'm as sad as you are about Dan," Marina said.

"Then you should be with us tomorrow," Paris insisted.

"Well, I can't," Marina said.

Paris pushed his chair away from the table and walked out of the room.

CHAPTER THIRTY SIX

P aris sat next to Helen. She wore her dark blue church dress with the white polka dots. Her hands in her lap looked small and childlike. Paris listened to the words about God and eternal rest, but nothing would stick with him like the thunder of the guns. Seven rifles and three volleys—the 21-gun salute. The *crack!* of each volley sounded like a rip in the fabric of the sky. Then, the bugler played *Taps,* and Helen started to cry softly. Paris swallowed his own grief so as to not add to hers.

Tommy and the officer in charge of the burial detail lifted the flag from the coffin and folded it precisely into a triangle of white stars on blue field. The officer presented it to Helen saying, "On behalf of the President of the United States, the Commandant of the Marine Corps, and a grateful nation, please accept this flag as a symbol of our appreciation for your son's service to Country and Corps."

Some of Helen's silver hair fell like a veil over her face as she looked up at him. This man had been with Dan in the war, and he leaned down to kiss her forehead. He whispered something.

Helen smiled and nodded. And so it went with a long line of men and women who paid their respects. Some left a flower or some other token on top of the casket. Tommy motioned for Paris to join him. From his pocket he withdrew a golf ball and tossed it into the grave. Paris took a pigeon feather from his pocket and dropped it in.

"This is our good friend Paris Thibideaux," Tommy said, putting his big hand on Paris's shoulder. Dan's friends and members of his family nodded and shook Paris's hand like he was a grown man. Grief was weighing on Tommy. His arms hung heavily at his sides, and his head seemed too heavy for his neck. But he took the time to introduce Paris to just about everyone. For the first time, Paris saw Dan's features on other faces. His eyes, especially, were everywhere among the Torvilson cousins, aunts and uncles. Surrounded by the Browneagle side of the family, Tommy looked more like Dan, too. Paris had never noticed before that when Tommy smiled, his face lit up in a particular way that was very similar to Dan's.

"Paris, let's help Aunt Helen back to the car," Tommy said, and Paris knew that he had found a place in this family. Helen rose out of her chair, cradling the flag in her arms.

"You ready, Aunt Helen?" Tommy asked.

Helen looked around, "Ya," she said, "I got the flag and *the stuff in here*," she said, tapping her heart, "thanks to all of you. God bless."

CHAPTER THIRTY SEVEN

Later that evening, when he was alone in his room, Paris thought about the funeral. He had never seen a real grave before. Adorned with flowers and suspended over a green-carpeted hole in the ground, the coffin was a jarring sight. No amount of flowers or green carpeting could disguise the fact that the box, with his friend in it, was going into the ground.

In the hollow of the night, Tommy carved out a place for himself. He had built a fire in an old 55-gallon oil drum, and the flames sent up sparks and smoke into the starry sky. He placed a hard-backed chair at the head of the putting green and faced the alley. Immediately before him was the ceremonial drum that had been in his family for generations. He took up the beaters and waited for the rhythm to come to him.

Dan and Tommy had spent so many hours over so many years in this back yard that tonight it seemed that all their various "selves" were there at once. Toddlers in a plastic wading pool. Boys climbing and falling out of trees. Teenagers sneaking out the back door. They were cousins who were more like brothers who were also friends.

The drum was old. The beaters were even older, but Tommy had wrapped the ends in new leather that made a crisp sound on the drumhead, a dancing sound that floated free and couldn't be bound to the earth. And then Tommy opened his mouth, and out came a voice from the beginning of time. It vibrated the bones of the face. It started as a seedling of sound, sprouting in the belly of the night. Bone song. The wail of chiefs and warriors. The grief of tribes. It reached Paris in his room. He hadn't cried at the funeral, but now he wept. Eventually, he drifted into a deep sleep.

Janos saw the sparks swirling upwards on invisible currents. Heavy-eyed and weary, he sat on his back porch—a half bottle of whiskey on the deck beside him—and latched on to the relentless, hollow, penetrating rhythm of the drum. It went straight to his chest and played on his ribs. Tommy's lamentation filled the air, and Janos felt his own grief stir within him, seeking a similar outlet, but there was no such bittersweet expression for all that he had lost, and alone in the night he came up wanting.

The plaintive wail of the mourning man evoked not just his loss, but the losses of generations. Primal loneliness of tribes wandering in the desert, forsaken by gods. But also the duty of the living to carry on, and to be the keepers of the song. Janos had become a frozen man who looked lifelike, but he was all sharp crystals and cutting edges inside. The drum drew him along like it was the spine of the universe; he couldn't get around it or over it. As the fire dwindled, the aromas of sage and tobacco drifted on the currents of night air. The old soldier who had died, the friend who mourned him, and the stranger listening in the dark might have talked together, raised a glass, smoked, and watched the sun set as old warriors have always done. But it was too late for that now. One of them had already moved on.

God! Your face should break before this song! Janos gulped the whiskey, which felt like ice and fire going down. How ironic to find himself talking to God—something he had vowed never to do again. Tommy's fire was down to embers now, and there was only the drum, and finally silence. Janos took another swig of whiskey and threw back his head as if to swallow the moon.

CHAPTER THIRTY EIGHT

Marina got home later than she had expected. She had worked a double-shift and now wondered if the extra money had been worth it. She was exhausted. When she looked in on Paris, he lay on his belly, his feet hanging over the side of the bed. She could see that already his arms and legs were too long for the pajamas she had bought last Christmas. She pulled the top sheet out from under and covered him, taking pains to do it gently so as not to wake him. But there was no chance of waking Paris from that sleep. Even when the lightning and thunder of a summer storm rolled in an hour later, he slept on oblivious.

Now it was her turn to fall into bed. She was exhausted and more than a little sick of herself. It had been a mistake to miss Dan's funeral. All day she had felt guilty about it, especially about sending Paris alone, and not being there for Helen, who had always been so kind. The double shift and the arduous work on the gutters all week-end had her muscles tied in knots. She tried doing a few stretches, but finally, she, too, fell into a deep sleep well before the storm hit.

Billy McNaughton, on the other hand, could not sleep at all. The approaching storm reminded him that he had work to do—what Ermler called "deconstruction." The storm would be the perfect cover for it, although it also made the job more dangerous.

When he got to the Thibideaux house, each stroke of lightning bathed the new gutters in a neon glow, followed by the rumble of thunder. He timed his movements to coincide with the thunder, beginning with the downspouts. All but one came down easily. He needed a ladder for the rest. Brazenly, he set up Marina's extension ladder, and armed with a claw hammer and a small crowbar, he climbed up and started ripping out the straps and fasteners that held the gutters. The rain began to come down in cold, heavy sheets as the storm intensified. Standing on an aluminum ladder touching metal to metal in the middle of an electrical storm, he knew, was crazy. But the danger only added to the excitement.

He had forgotten to wear gloves, and one of the fastenings did not want to let go. Using his bare fingers, he tried to pry it loose. Because of the cold and the dark, he didn't even realize he was bleeding until a flash of lightning lit up his hand. Then, it hurt. There was nothing to do but keep going. It wasn't easy. The cut slashed across three fingers, so there was no way to grasp the ladder or a tool without pain.

In the torrential rain, the ground was turning to pudding. It sucked at his sneakers and the feet of the ladder. But Billy plodded on in spite of the wind, the cold rain, the mud, the pain, and the locomotive noise and speed of the storm. Billy had to work fast to keep up with it. Finally, he was running through the morning mist toward home, his hands and arms bruised and bloody, and he was soaked and chilled to the bone. Working for Felix Ermler was like wading in sewage, he thought, and going home was not much better. His heart sank with every step that brought him closer to his father's house. It struck him like a blow that no matter what he did to the Thibideaux house, his own house was still a hellhole. No matter what he did to Paris, that boy still had a mother who loved him.

Harold McNaughton's heavy snoring announced his presence in the darkened house. The smell of liquor, cigarettes, and body odors permeated the living room where the old man had passed out. Billy slipped past the sleeping hulk on the floor and went up to his room.

He stripped off his wet clothes and dove under the covers. His flesh was as cold and hard as stone. Downstairs, his father snorted loudly, belched and swore in his sleep. The sun seeped into his room around the edges of the old paper shades that Billy always kept pulled down over his windows. He thrust his head under his pillow. That was better. Now, all he had to deal with was the realization that what he *really* hated was *not* Paris Thibideaux. It was simply everything.

CHAPTER THIRTY NINE

Paris lurched down the stairs and careened into the kitchen. Marina was pacing the perimeter of the room like a caged animal.

"Yes, Mr. Ermler, I installed them myself! What does that have to do with anything? Somebody tore them all down . . . everything!"

Paris ran past her out the back door. The new gutters lay in twisted piles as though a giant had ripped them away from the house and stomped on them.

"Storm damage!" she exclaimed biting her lip to keep from interrupting him, but it was impossible.

"They didn't *fall* down. They were ripped down!"

Paris couldn't understand who would be so bold and so malicious toward them? Or why?

"I don't know WHO!" Marina growled.

Paris walked around the corner of the house, but he could still hear her.

"I need more time to finish," she was pleading now, "could you please back off just a little? I'll pay part at the end of the month, and the rest when I get the loan."

Paris could hear the panic growing in her voice, and it was clear that Ermler was being unsympathetic or stupid or both.

"Mr. Ermler, that is not true," she said slamming her fist into something that made the silverware rattle, "The contract does not *require* you to do this. You *could* let me finish the work and pay you off."

Paris stood by a downspout that had been twisted like a giant pipe cleaner and listened through the open window, as his mother's voice got smaller and smaller until she practically whispered something she didn't want him to hear.

"Okay, I'm *begging* now for my son's sake."

She had lowered herself into a chair and closed her eyes, but she could still hear herself begging, as she had never done before. Paris heard, too, and all the hope that they had lived on for as long as he could remember, suddenly vaporized and was gone. He felt for his mother, and he knew he was the only one who could help her now. He had grown up a lot over the past few weeks, and he didn't like it much. No matter who had done what, or why they had done it, there was a mess to clean up; and, it was the Thibideaux's mess, fair or not.

Marina hung up the phone and went outside, where the devastation hit her all over again.

"I can't believe this," she murmured, as she sat down on the steps and covered her face with her hands. In the dark world behind her eyes, she was an utter failure. *I can't keep anything. I will never keep anything. Husband. Money. House.* And then, she thought of Paris, and the thought of losing him was overwhelming.

Paris could hear her sobbing, but he felt driven to keep doing what he was doing. He was sifting out the junk and making a pile of reusable materials. Somehow, it seemed more important than comforting her with kind words and hugs. In a way, he was right. The sound of metal clanking against metal caught her attention. She wiped her face and followed the sound. On the side of the house, she found Paris sorting.

He smiled at the sight of her coming toward him. He had been afraid that Ermler had finally worn her down. Now, although she looked more fragile than ever, she was pleasantly surprised to see him working.

"What do you think?" he asked, holding up a piece of downspout.

She picked up another piece saying, "Looks like there's a lot we can reuse."

"Let's call this the useable pile," Paris said, picking up a length of gutter and placing it with other similar pieces.

Marina set down a twisted length of metal and said, "And this is the hopeless pile."

Paris could see that she was coming back from whatever Hell, Ermler and the Gutter Bandit had tried to send her to.

CHAPTER FORTY

I t was definitely Parade Season in Powderhorn, and the boundar-
ies between work and play, childhood and adulthood, had melted
away. It was hard to find a yard that wasn't the site of some kind of
float construction, juggling practice, or dance rehearsal. Even the
animals got in on it. Two Ton and some of the other dogs had put
themselves on "dropped-food" patrol, occasionally helping toddlers
who didn't know when to let go of their snacks. Within this bubble of
cheery confusion, the Thibideaux house stood apart. With a mountain of physical labor in front of them, there was still a deep canyon
of uncertainty ahead. Ermler had refused to back off from his deadline, and that meant that Marina would have to take more days out of
Paris's childhood to make him work like a man. Yet, they were doing
well together. Yesterday, she and Paris laid out all the gutters that were
still useable, and Marina had just enough credit to buy the pieces she
needed to fill in the gaps. As the morning wore on, and they fell into
the routine of working together, Paris couldn't stop thinking about
the work he wished he were doing on his parade horse. Time was running out. He felt the same urgency as everyone else in the neighborhood, but right now his mother needed him more.

Ironically, Paris and Marina did not *appear* to be as out-of-step with their neighbors as they felt. So many back yards were in an uproar that the clutter of the Thibideaux yard did not stand out. Still, Marina felt keenly the difference between her task and everyone else's, and though she kept it to herself, she wished she could be across the alley with Mrs. Vang, helping to build a dragon from a sea of bright silks. They both hunkered down and did what they had to do—the less said, the better. Back and forth they went up the ladder to the edge of the roof and down again for more supplies. Suddenly, the gate swung open, and Janos Kovac came into the yard. He looked as though he had just fallen out of bed after a particularly bad night—spiky hair, unshaven face, rumpled clothes. Marina recognized a hangover when she saw one, but Paris believed that Janos had come to help.

"Wow! You're here!" he gushed.

"Yes, I am," Janos said, stumbling back a step. On seeing Marina striding toward him, he straightened up and made a half-hearted attempt to iron his clothes with his hands.

"What do you want?" Marina demanded, "You don't look so good."

"I come to . . ." he began, but when he looked into her eyes, he lost the thread, "Are you putting up or tearing down? Is hard to tell . . ." he asked, looking around.

"Both," Paris offered.

Janos stared at him blankly.

Marina cleared her throat, and this seemed to bring him back, "I came to get my drill. I forgot I don't like to lend tools."

"Paris, where's his drill?" Marina interrupted, "We don't like to borrow tools."

"But I was going to . . ." Paris began.

"Yeah, you were going to return it, but you forgot!" Janos interjected, and then turning to Marina, he added, "He lives with his head in the clouds."

"He's a child," Marina snapped, "something you probably don't understand."

She was just being flip, but this seemed to hit him unusually hard. Sensing that she had hit a nerve, Marina continued with more restraint, "Look, he'll bring you the drill later. Maybe you should go home now."

"But Mom, he came to help!" Paris still clung to a faint hope that it all might still work out.

"No!" Janos shook his head emphatically, "I am not here to help anyone."

"But, I . . ." Paris began.

"Get it through your head," Janos said sternly, "you and me—we are not friends!"

"What is wrong with you? Don't talk to him like that!" Marina cried.

He looked at her, and she thought he had the saddest eyes in the world. But when he spoke, she was sure she had imagined it.

"What do you care? You are never here," he said accusingly, "He follows me—at work, at home."

Sad or not, she let him have it, "I care that you're drunk and you're mean, but for some reason, my son looks up to you!"

"I am not a babysitter!" Janos exclaimed.

"That's it!" Marina snapped, "Get out!"

"Look, lady," Janos said deliberately, "maybe he need somebody, but is not me."

"Why would anybody need you?" Marina exploded, "You're as useless as a stray dog!"

"I'd rather be stray dog than you right now," he shot back.

"Stop!" Paris cried, but Janos had locked eyes with Marina, and he was not about to hold back.

"You run around here desperate like you are losing the world, but what are you losing? A house! And only because you made a stupid deal with the Devil, you . . . you are a silly woman with too much hair!"

Janos pointed to Paris, "You should be teaching him not to believe his own fairy tales."

"You're drunk, and I don't want you here," Marina said, struggling to hold on to her emotions. But her obvious anger brought a crooked smile to Janos's face that was meant to goad her. Marina recognized that kind of smile. It was the mask of toughness that people wear to hide their pain. And for the second time, she sensed the man's profound sadness, even though his meanness was inexcusable.

"Just bring me the drill when you find it," he said to Paris as he left.

Marina slammed the gate after him and turned to Paris, "Stay away from that man!" she said sternly.

"OK," Paris said.

"And give back his damn drill!"

"OK," he repeated.

"Do you hear me?" she demanded.

"Yes!" he shouted.

Now that they had stopped yelling at each other, their attention was drawn to the alley, and the spectacle of Janos Kovac with arms outstretched to the sky, "You clownish people, with your puppets and your floats! What you need is all Hell to break loose to teach you a lesson!" Between the music and the construction noise, nobody was listening but Marina and Paris, who watched as Janos stumbled the rest of the way home.

CHAPTER FORTY ONE

The house was dark, and they had been asleep for hours when he was awakened by the distinct sound of shattering glass.

"Did you hear that?" Paris called out to his mother as he jumped out of bed.

"Yes!" Marina shouted, taking the stairs two at a time right behind Paris. In the kitchen smoke drifted in through the window screens, confirming that they weren't dreaming. Paris threw open the back door, but all he could see was a wall of fire. Black plumes of smoke churned above the burning garage and blocked out the night sky.

Mesmerized, Paris stepped on to the porch and into the intense heat thrown off by the blaze. Molten bits of the roof flew up into the atmosphere and fell back to earth still burning. The roar of the hungry fire drew an anguished cry from Marina as she pulled Paris back from the edge of the steps and held him. They watched in silence as the fire bore down like a beast breaking the back of its prey. The crackle of burning wood sounded like crunching bones, or rapid gunfire. Red tongues of flame licked the walls and blasted through the top of the cupola. The roof was a glowing mesh of red-hot coals and undulating like a sail lifted by unseen currents. Sirens, already too late, screamed in the distance. Suddenly, the roof heaved up in the middle with a sickly groan, and the entire structure began to fold in on itself.

Marina's hair had come loose, and her wet face glistened in the eerie light. The back wall came crashing down first. The alley wall was next. Marina buried her face in Paris's shoulder, but Paris couldn't take his eyes from the wall directly in front of them. Behind it, was something that mattered only to him. The wall was nothing but a charred lace curtain with no visible means of support. It came down almost gracefully, like the final curtain of an opera; and, there, standing defiant within the inferno—glowing red-hot like a torch— was the horse. In the bluish beams of light thrown by the fire trucks, and framed by sweeping arcs of water, its terrible beauty stopped all mouths. Even the firefighters ceased giving orders and stared. Marina turned to her son, "Paris?"

CHAPTER FORTY TWO

The sun rose in an ashen sky. Greasy soot clung to every leaf and surface, turning the landscape into a grainy black-and-white ghost image washed of almost all color. Paris stood before the ruins of his garage. It was rubble now, with the charred remains of the cupola perched on top like a perverse party hat. Everything was coated with a mix of ash and chemicals. Black particles, micro-cinders, circulated in the air all around him and carried the sour smell of the after-fire into his nose and throat.

In the middle of it all, the horse stood exposed, and it might as well have been Paris's heart, for all to see. The fire had turned the garage inside out, and what had been private was suddenly as public as the city dump. He looked toward Dan's porch, knowing it would be empty, and squeezed the grip of the long-handled putter he had made for him just a few weeks ago. Maybe, Dan could have made sense out this destruction, but Dan was gone.

Paris started to climb the mountain of waterlogged debris, using the putter to probe and poke around the spongy wet mass underfoot. Suddenly, he took a swing at a can that contained scorched bird feathers and sent it flying. It was as if the fire had leapt into Paris and was still smoldering within him. Fire is a chemical process that rearranges things at the deep molecular level. Once the chemical reactions in a fire get going, they are almost impossible to stop. The heat of the flame keeps the fuel in a state of ignition as long as there is fuel and oxygen around it. The burning fuel releases gases, and the flame ignites the gases as well. The fire spreads until there is nothing left for it to burn, or until it is extinguished by cutting off its oxygen.

"Hey, Swamp Boy. You finally burned down your garage! What an idiot . . ." Billy McNaughton laughed as he turned his bike in disturbingly tight circles.

Paris's blood froze, and his grip tightened on the putter. He couldn't believe so many bad things could happen all at the same time.

"Welcome to my world, man. Shit happens! And speakin' of crap, what were you building in there. A cow? Mooooooo!"

Looking down, Paris calculated how many strides it would take him to reach Billy. Four, maybe five.

"Your mom's *really* got her ass in a sling now!" Billy howled, spinning recklessly.

The bike wobbled, and Paris sprang for him. There was no thought behind it, only raw energy. The long-handled putter sliced the air like a helicopter blade, knocking the rear wheel of Billy's bike out from under him. Billy toppled to the ground pinned by the bike. Paris bashed the rear wheel again and then the front one, making Billy squirm in a state of terror. Paris lifted the bike and heaved it aside. He rested the edge of the putter against Billy's nose.

"You want to say something else about my mother, Asshole?" Paris roared.

He slid the putter across Billy's face and down to his ear, "Where's *your* mother, Bill? Oh, yeah! She took off! How sad is that?"

Paris had never felt the thrill of revenge. There was an unexpected and hideous pleasure in standing over Billy and making him feel weak and afraid. He raised the putter high above his head and brought it down with all of his might first on one side, and then on the other side of Billy's head again and again, rendering Billy a cringing, blubbering lump on the ground. Suddenly, someone grabbed him and ripped the putter from his hands. He heard it land with a thud in his yard.

"Let me go!" Paris cried.

"Run, boy!" Janos roared at Billy.

Paris struggled to break Janos's hold, as Billy, still shaken, roused himself and staggered away.

"I'll kill you, Billy!" Paris shrieked, breaking free.

Janos caught him again and grumbled hoarsely, "Stop, damn it, you don't know what you say!"

Paris wilted.

"Hey! You okay?" Janos asked. Paris looked as though he had fainted, but his body was as tense as a coiled spring. Janos asked again, "Answer me. You okay now?"

Paris nodded.

"Good," Janos said and loosened his grip.

Paris rounded on him and landed his fist on Janos's jaw. They both cried out in pain. Janos seized him in a headlock.

"I can't breathe," Paris gasped, "I'm gonna be sick."

"Okay, okay, I don't want to hurt you," Janos let go. Paris responded this time with a blow to Janos's ribs.

"Ohhhh!" cried Janos, doubling over as Paris collapsed in a heap, "What the hell you doing? You think I let you kill this boy?"

"What the hell *you* doing?" Paris shot back, "Why don't you go back where you came from?"

"Can't," Janos said, offering a hand to help him up, but Paris got to his feet on his own.

"What good are you?" Paris spat contemptuously, "You're useless."

Janos threw up his hands, "I couldn't watch you do this! You don't know . . ."

Paris climbed the mountain of rubble and waded into the ashes. He wanted to sink down where it was cool and pungent, and lonely, and the world was the color of nothing. He began to dance on the grave of the garage, scooping up fistfuls of ashes and throwing them into the air. Using his bare hands, he covered himself with ashes, trying to erase himself from the world.

Janos could only watch from the alley as the dust enveloped Paris. How well he knew the taste of ashes! Paris raised up a gray cloud, and when it cleared, he was gone.

CHAPTER FORTY THREE

The neighborhood reacted to the fire like a death in the family. They put parade preparations on hold. Throughout the day, friends came to the back door and left food. They understood that Marina might not come out and take it right away, but they kept bringing it anyway. As Randi said, "That's what Tupperware is for."

Many of them knew Felix Ermler well enough to know that he would find a way to profit from the fire. Smaller disasters had befallen other tenants who wouldn't go quietly when he pulled the plug on their contracts. Until now, however, no one had ever fought so hard and so well as Marina. The question of the hour was: had Felix Ermler felt compelled to escalate to the point of destroying a piece of his own property; and, if so, that meant that he was also willing to put the neighbors' houses at risk. For these and other reasons of common decency, the friends of the Thibideaux's who lived up and down the alley, became more vigilant. The safety of the neighborhood had been compromised, and now the fire was everybody's business.

All morning they gathered around the fallen garage, speaking in reverent tones occasionally punctuated by the kind of laugh you hear at a wake when people recall something humorous about the departed. And they discovered things about Paris that might have remained hidden, or at least private, but for the fire: that their trash had become his treasure, and that the anonymous repair jobs being done on both sides of the alley, were anonymous no more. Paris's cover had been blown.

But as significant and moving as these discoveries were to Paris's friends, the iron horse was the fire's most startling revelation. It drew hushed reverence and awe. Within hours, it had drawn people from several blocks away to come and see it. Max's wife, Solveigh, resting her hand gently on the horse's neck as though it were alive, was the first to say what the others were thinking, "I guess we always knew that Paris sees things different than we do."

"Paris is a shepherd of *things*," Blossum said quietly, "and God loves a shepherd."

"He's an artist." Pete said, removing his ball cap.

Meanwhile, Paris had retreated to his room with the curtains drawn against the light of day. Darkness had entered his heart, and taken over all of his thoughts, turning everything good into its opposite. Paris reeked of the sharp, sour smell of the fire just like everything else that it had consumed. A glimpse of himself in the mirror confirmed that, like a lump of metal in Blossum's forge, he had been transformed. He wasn't a flesh-and-blood-boy, but a ghost boy who came from ashes. *Be yourself, Paris, no matter what.* Dan's words came back to haunt him as he held the putter in his hands.

In the bathroom, he scrubbed at the grease and soot until his skin was red and raw. He changed into clean clothes, but when he was done, nothing had changed on the inside. The putter lay on his dresser, wiped clean, but there was no escaping that he had turned a gift into a weapon. In his heart, where Dan was alive, he was ashamed. *You can't let a bully scare you out of being who you are, who you were meant to be,* Dan had said. But Billy knew the truth the moment he saw Paris that morning: that his soul was up for grabs.

"Welcome to *my* world!" Billy said, and just like that, Paris gave himself over to the glamour of evil—instant gratification; the settling of all scores; the end of all empathy and responsibility; and the dark excitement of revenge. In the grip of his anger, he felt justified in doing anything. The bruises on his knuckles proved that he had really struck the hard jaw of a grown man. POW! It had felt good to hit Janos for being mean and for rejecting his friendship. For Paris, Janos was standing in for all the fathers who ever walked away from their children. POW! But Paris had no way of knowing that he was punishing a man who was already punishing himself—a man doomed to wander alone for the rest of his life.

Janos had taken the punch square in the jaw, and it had rattled him. He recognized in Paris something of himself, and therefore something of his sons. They had been brutally killed, and Janos struggled to keep those memories at bay by avoiding children and, if necessary, actively trying to repel them. He didn't want to remember that he had ever been a father. Only Paris Thibideaux was not put off by his Mean Old Man routine. The boy had landed a surprisingly good shot to his chin, and Janos thought the Mean Old Man in him sorely deserved it. But it was the father in him that had saved Paris from doing something terrible. That made him feel good—proud even—that he still had the impulse to do something instead of turning away. Now, he was in the crowd that had gathered in the Thibideaux back yard, and he agreed with Pete that Paris was indeed an artist.

"Yes," he said, standing by the horse's head and touching its muzzle, "I have seen this before, sculpture from scrap metal."

He examined it closely, grasping the ribs and joints. The cold metal was solidly welded, but the horse was beautifully proportioned and appeared to step lightly. He ran his hand along the horse's neck and spine.

"This is rudimentary armature with some excellent welding. Quite amazing, actually. I would never guess he was capable of this."

"He must've used my equipment to do it, too," Pete said, turning to Blossum, "the sneaky little genius. I always knew he was our main competition."

"Yeah, yeah. You're clairvoyant," Blossum said, "but Felix Ermler is gonna swoop in here any minute and take everything."

"He will still do this?" Janos asked, looking around and seeing general agreement, he continued, "Then, we must begin with cleanup. Save what can be saved, and pitch what can be pitched."

If Hope is a dozen or so people who can't wait to fix something even though they don't know how, then Hope was alive in Powderhorn; and, it was infectious. A pool of shovels, brooms, and trash bags developed, as people fell to cleaning up. Suddenly, *expectation* was in the air.

As the day wore on, Janos was still a man of few words, still for the most part a solitary man in the middle of a crowd, but he was moving along with the tide of humanity, which he hadn't done in a long, long time. It occurred to him that perhaps God's face had not turned away from *all* the children.

CHAPTER FORTY FOUR

When Paris came into the room, Marina was standing over the kitchen sink, looking like she was going to be sick.

"Are you all right?" he asked.

"The bank won't approve the loan we need to pay off Ermler," she said without lifting her head.

"What?"

"Mr. Holmgren called. He's already heard about the fire and without the garage, he can't . . ." her voice caught in her throat. She swallowed hard and continued, "We need to start packing."

"No!" Paris cried.

"Yes!" Marina bellowed, pounding her fist on the counter, "I quit!"

Paris stared at her in disbelief as she sent a stack of clean dishes and bowls flying off the counter. They hit the floor and shattered noisily. She pulled out a drawer, sending the silverware clanging to the floor. One glass remained in the sink. She picked it up and held it up over her head.

"What are you doing?" Paris cried, reaching for the glass.

"The dishes," she said, opening her hand and letting the glass fall fatally to the floor. She kicked aside the shards and strode into the living room.

"Mom, stop it!" Paris protested.

She threw couch pillows, magazines, and even tools into the large trash bin she kept in the center of the living room for construction debris. Paris pulled the circular saw out of the trash while she turned her attention to kicking apart a stack of lumber. He stepped into her path.

"Get out of my way!" she hissed.

"You're destroying everything!" Paris shouted.

Defiantly, she picked up a claw hammer and sank its head into a new section of drywall.

"Don't *ever* say that to me!" she sputtered, sinking the claw into another spot and then another. She kicked over a box of ten-penny nails and sent them jingling across the floor, "I *built* this! And I can wreck it!"

"I built it, too!"

"I mean it, MOVE!" she yelled in his face, and suddenly something snapped within Paris.

"You know what, Mom?" Paris said, stepping aside, "Go for it. Murder it."

Marina eyed him warily.

"Go ahead," he said, "but don't expect any help from me."

She slapped him. Tears of outrage rose to his eyes, and in an instant he was out the door, slamming it behind him.

"Go ahead! Walk away, just like your father!" she screamed.

He found that he had stepped into a small mountain of food containers on the back porch. Also, half the neighborhood had gathered in his back yard. They must have heard everything, and like him, they must be able to hear Marina still tearing the place apart, but they were too polite to let on.

"Damn!" she cried out, and Paris knew that she must have hurt herself because that was the only time she swore. He felt no sympathy. She always said, "If you work mad, you get hurt."

As he looked out over the yard, his heart sank at the sight of his horse—standing naked, up to its knees in burnt trash with a crowd of people milling about. He sat down on the bottom step, wishing he could disappear, but where to? He felt like he didn't belong anywhere. For the moment, he was invisible. All attention was focused on the Hoistabus. Pete was backing it up to the part of the one wall that was still standing. The engine whined and strained until the wall came crashing down. Dust rose, and dust settled. Almost instantly, the cleanup resumed.

"Save as much as you can, people," Randi commanded. She looked toward the house, and gave Paris a nod. Others turned and did the same, but then quickly went back to work. Paris looked away. So much had happened in the past few hours that he felt twisted and jumbled inside. He wasn't sure what would come out if he opened his mouth. Who would speak: Paris or the Ghost Boy of the Ashes? He needed to find a safe haven. Sanctuary. As quickly as it dawned on him, he was up and over the fence.

Zippo was on the couch, lying in Dan's spot, as though he'd been waiting for him. Paris sat down and rested his hand on the cat's back. The putting green was still there, a little overgrown and weedy since Tommy went up North after the funeral. The coffee can was still nailed to the porch rail, but Helen had emptied and cleaned it. The small refrigerator had been emptied of all beer and unplugged, but Dan's bag of golf clubs was still in the corner, leaned against the house. Paris rested his head on the big over-stuffed cushions, and let his gaze fall on his own yard next door. He tried to see his neighbors the way Dan would have seen them—coming together like a team that needed no coach, but it was no use. He closed his eyes so he wouldn't have to look at them rifling through his things. Soon, he realized that he was not alone. He recognized the voices, but he kept his eyes closed against Pete and Blossum.

"Helen said Dan kept his toolbox here on the porch, but I don't see it," Blossum said, climbing the steps.

Pete stood at the bottom of the steps, "I bet Paris knows where it is."

Without even opening his eyes, Paris said, "I came here to be by myself."

Blossum sat down heavily on the couch, "You see what's goin' on at *your* house?"

"Yeah: bunch of busybodies going through my stuff. I wish they'd knock it off," Paris said.

"Nobody's going through your stuff, man," Pete said, "we're trying to clear the way for a *new* garage. We want to help you stay."

"It's not gonna happen," Paris said coldly.

"We're just giving it a try," Blossum said, rising, "'though it looks like you've given up."

"Get off my back! I'm sick of this whole neighborhood. I hate it, I hate the park, and I hate the parade! None of it is working for me, okay? So just get out of my face!"

Blossum and Pete looked at each other, and Blossum said, "You know, it's not just you and your mom losing something here."

"It's all of us," Pete added.

"Yeah, what are *you* gonna lose?" Paris asked pointedly.

"Think about it," Blossum retorted.

"Everybody in this alley has had some bad times," Pete said softly, "You're old enough to understand that, Paris."

"Leave me alone," Paris said bitterly.

Pete took off his cap and scratched his head.

"Come on, Pete," Blossum said, descending the steps, "I thought I saw Paris over here, but I guess not."

They were halfway to the gate when Paris got up and lifted the seat cushion, reached into the cavity, and pulled out a big green toolbox.

"Hey!" he called after them, "Just take it and don't pester me anymore."

Blossum turned, crossed his big arms and stared at Paris, "Not like that, man. I will not have it."

Finally, Paris said, "*Please* take it."

"Well, then," Blossum said, returning to the porch, "thank you."

He took the box and said to Pete, "Let's leave this young man to his meditations.

CHAPTER FORTY FIVE

Off they went, slope-shouldered and clearly disappointed. Even Zippo looked disgusted. It was nonsense, Paris told himself, to think that Zippo had an opinion, but the cat let out a raspy, complaining meow. Suddenly, a chill seized him. *Don't do this here. This is no hideout!* Paris looked around. He wasn't sure if he'd actually heard the words. It might have been Dan's voice, or his own conscience, but it made him stand up and look around. He had no idea where in the world he could go now to feel safe. The garage had been a sanctuary; it was gone. The house had been "home;" it was being taken away. Dan had been his friend in times of need; he was gone now, too. He went through the gate that he had repaired with the tiny truck wheels just a few weeks ago. So much had changed since then.

His own yard was overrun with men, women, and children—all of them wielding brooms, shovels, rakes, or trash bags—being careful not to look in his direction. They seemed to know that he needed at least the illusion of privacy, and he began to think more kindly of them. They had moved his horse into the yard. It was clear that they were not just cleaning up. Even Janos was taking measurements of the perimeter of the old garage. *If he's out there*... Paris thought, recalling that the last time he was with Janos, he had punched him in the face.

He stayed in the alley for a long time, just watching, but he knew it was never going to get any easier. He entered the yard like a diver taking the plunge. There was no time to reflect. Max was there in an instant, greeting him with a pat on his back; Pete and Blossum each shook his hand; then Randi and Helen hugged him. And so it went with neighbor after neighbor welcoming him back as if he'd been away for a long time, and he accepted these gestures graciously, like the dutiful son at a funeral. Finally, Janos came forward and put out his hand. Paris did not shrink from looking him in the eye, but he couldn't help noticing some swelling in the area of Janos's jaw. Janos handed him a hammer. Gratefully, Paris took it. Clearly, Janos trusted him, and he could trust himself.

The next day volunteer scavengers went out looking for building materials, and by the end of the day they had acquired stacks of old sheet metal, a wooden door, and two sets of storm windows. Max had rented a dumpster, and the Hoistabus was being used to lift and dump the heavy loads. By the third day, framing had begun with lumber paid for by Helen Torvilson with money left in Dan's savings account, and Pete donated an old side panel from the Hoistabus to be part of the new and improved garage. Still, there was no coordinated design and no management to speak of. The project was just growing willy-nilly, fueled by tons of good intentions and not a drop of architectural restraint.

Predictably, relationships began to fray. Tools were dropped, toes were stubbed, and tempers flared. The ultimate explosion started out innocently enough when Pete got trigger-happy with the nail gun and accidentally nailed Blossum's shirt to a stud. In retaliation, Blossum tore the cigar from between Pete's teeth, and stomped it to flinders. Randi got between the two of them.

"That's it!" she said, "The tail's been waggin' this dog too long. *Somebody's* gotta take charge."

She was only saying what everyone else was thinking, and all eyes converged on Janos. He put up his hands, "No, no, no! You don't know what you're asking."

The silent appeal of all those eyes was hard to resist.

"All right!" he capitulated, "but I warn you: I am not good with people who don't listen. I yell."

"Honey!" Randi retorted, "we *all* yell!"

For days Marina went to work and came home by way of the front door, while Paris came and went by way of the back door. They barely spoke and they didn't eat together, either. Paris had company and plenty of hard work all day long, but for Marina, the isolation was torture. She was alone with her thoughts, even at work. She had started packing and began looking for an apartment. All she found were a couple of dumps, and she cried after looking over each one. As much as she missed Paris, she was angry with him too, for defying and abandoning her to handle this hateful move by herself. She had expected him to tire of his rebellion by now, and the neighbors to have quit by now, too; but, they were still out there all day and into the night.

On the afternoon of the third day, after extra long overtime at work, Marina was alone in the kitchen. She happened to have a frying pan in her hand when the voices, and especially the laughter, coming from the yard, pushed her over the edge. She appeared on the back porch and banged the bottom of the cast-iron pan on the porch rail until she had everyone's attention. She was not prepared for the sight now before her. Not only was the new garage far from finished, but it wasn't even square. For "siding," they had used sheet metal, plywood, an old green highway sign with giant arrows, and side paneling from Pete's green bus. Randi came forward, and Marina spoke directly to her at first.

"I want to thank you for all the food you gave us, but . . ."

A chorus of jovial voices sang out, "You're welcome!"

Lifting her eyes to take in the whole crowd, she began again slowly and deliberately, "BUT! The fire was the end for us. So, everybody, go home!"

"Well, at least you're taking it lying down," Randi said dryly.

"Really, Randi?" Marina sighed, crossing her arms so she'd have some place to tuck in her trembling hands, "Why don't you stop making a party out of my mess?"

There was a low rumble of discontent and then complete silence.

"Now," Marina continued, "where's Paris? I need to talk to my son."

"In there," Randi said, wagging her thumb in the direction of the garage.

CHAPTER FORTY SIX

S parks rained down around Pete as he tried to weld an old side panel of his green bus to a metal post connected to the framing of the garage wall.

"I'm not getting' it!" he exclaimed from his precarious position atop a stepladder, "Turn off the juice and spot me now, I'm comin' down."

Blossum disconnected the clamps from the terminals on the Juice Cart, and Paris steadied the ladder. Pete came down in a huff. When he had both feet on the ground again, he pulled off his helmet and declared, "It's too tight up there. I'm makin' a mess."

"Maybe, this bus-wall thing can't be done," Janos suggested.

"I can do it," Paris said.

"No!" Blossum said, "We don't need to antagonize you mother any more than we already have."

"I've done harder stuff than that," Paris insisted.

"I say we give it a whirl," Pete said as he handed over his helmet and gloves to Paris. We can't go treatin' him like a kid anymore!"

"But he *is* a kid—no offense, Paris," Blossum said earnestly.

"He's an artist," Pete corrected him, and Blossum's eyes rolled in exasperation.

"Give me five minutes," Paris said, donning the helmet and gloves. Blossum nodded resignedly.

"Turn the Juice Cart back on," Pete said to Janos.

Janos circled the wagon warily.

"I've used it before. Stop worrying," Paris said in a voice muffled by the helmet.

"Blossum, are you sure this is safe?" Janos asked earnestly.

"Yeah, he's got the touch," Blossum said, "you watch."

Paris climbed the ladder and went to work. DZZZT! Sparks burst from the wand. DZZZT! DZZZT! The Juice Cart hummed and vibrated. All three men were completely absorbed in watching Paris do with ease what Pete couldn't.

"You IDIOTS!" Marina exclaimed, rushing toward the ladder.

Blossum intercepted her, "We'll get him down for you. Take it easy."

Marina paced and muttered under her breath until Paris had both feet on the floor. Pete smiled sheepishly as he helped Paris remove the helmet and gloves. He squinted up and pointed to the work Paris had just done.

"He does a beautiful job, just beautiful!"

"Are you *trying* to kill my son?" Marina demanded.

"Please, Mrs. . . . ." Janos began.

Marina's eyes drilled into Paris, "Get in the house!"

"No!" Paris shouted, looking from Pete to Blossum to Janos for support.

"Don't look at them!" Marina commanded, "I'm your mother!"

"And they're my *friends*!" Paris interjected.

"And *you*!" Marina turned her fury on Janos, "what are *you* doing here? I distinctly remember you telling my son that you were NOT his friend."

Janos scratched his ear and said, "I change my mind."

Marina grabbed Paris's shirtsleeve, but he broke away from her. She glared at the men, "Do you think this is good—that my son doesn't listen to me?"

They avoided her eyes and sheepishly studied their feet. Finally, Janos spoke, "Paris, you must go with your mother."

Then, looking directly at Marina, he added, "For respect."

When he looked to Pete and Blossum for support, Paris recognized from the looks on their faces that he had lost this round. For a moment, relief turned up the corners of Marina's stern mouth. Janos took note of a slight tremor in her hand as she laid it on Paris's shoulder. He sensed that it was her heart and not her pride that suffered now. The three men followed them out of the garage and into the sunlit yard. Helen Torvilson reached out to put her arm around Marina's shoulder.

"Marina, can we talk?" Helen asked. Marina shrugged her off coldly. Helen looked to Paris and Janos and said, "Why don't you boys find some work to do. I'll talk to her now."

Paris motioned to Pete and Janos, and they walked toward the house quickly.

"Do *not* go into my house!" Marina cried.

Helen put her hands firmly on Marina's shoulders, "You need to listen to your friends, now."

"If you were really my friends," Marina said, searching the faces surrounding her, "you'd show some respect, and leave us alone!"

"We are showing respect," Helen countered, "for Paris."

"You're not his mother, Helen!" Marina said, her voice shaking, "This is my family! Butt out!"

Then she turned to everyone gathered in her yard, "You should all go home. It's over . . . please go!"

Suddenly Blossum bounded past Marina and up the steps to where Paris was holding open the screen door.

"Hey!" Marina ran up the steps and reached for the door, but Paris blocked it.

"Mom," he said cheerfully, "it's gonna be good. Honest. Just give us a few minutes."

Marina looked into his earnest face, and exhaustion took over, "Oh, Paris, all right. A few minutes, but when I come in there, what I say, goes."

"Okay!" Paris said, disappearing inside.

Marina turned to Helen, "You know, he *believes* it's 'gonna be good,' but he's still a child."

Helen said, "You have been given many gifts, Marina, and most of them are right here with you now. How you receive them and appreciate them, especially Paris, is up to you."

"Helen, you don't know what you're talking about."

She opened the screen door and went inside.

CHAPTER FORTY SEVEN

The anger that had swept her into the house like a monsoon wind had dissipated, leaving her with a vague pain in her head and a tightness in her chest. She stood in her own kitchen, rubbing her temples and listening to Paris in the living room explaining the header problem, and all she had done so far to correct it, as clearly and accurately as she had once explained it to him. Nevertheless, she couldn't allow these men to peddle false hope to her son. She moved silently into the edge of the living room, watching and listening. Janos was running his hand over the holes in the wall that she had made with the claw hammer. He stopped as soon as he saw that Marina was watching him. She picked up a push broom and entered the room.

"I'd like you all to leave now," she said, "I need to talk with my son."

"But Mom," Paris began.

Blossum said, "Marina, we could . . ."

"Please! It's hard enough without all of you filling his head with nonsense!" she interrupted, and then to Pete, she added, "You should be ashamed of yourself, Pete Chavez. You put an eleven-year-old boy on top of a rickety ladder with an arc welder!"

"Wasn't rickety," Janos said.

"What?"

"Wasn't rickety, we were holding it," he replied.

Marina squinted at him skeptically, "Oh, thank you Mr. *You-Should-Teach-Your-Son-Not-To-Believe-In-Fairy-Tales!*"

"I was wrong," Janos retorted.

"No kidding. Now, get out!" Marina snapped.

"Mom!" Paris exclaimed.

"No!" Janos held up his hands, "She says go, we should go! Is her house."

Blossum nodded, and Pete looked deflated.

Paris turned to Janos, "But *I* say you should stay!"

"Boy," Janos said wearily, "we do as your mother says."

As Pete and Blossum headed for the back door, Janos took a step closer to Marina and said quietly, "I am sorry for that day I came into the yard so . . ."

"Drunk," Marina said.

Janos recoiled, "I would say angry."

"I would say drunk," Marina insisted.

"Yes, okay, *drunk*," he said, inclining to speak softly and directly to her, "point is: I said things that were stupid."

They seemed to have forgotten that Paris was still in the room. He saw his mother's expression soften, as looked up at him.

"It doesn't matter now," she said, "The bank said no."

"Oh, I didn't know," Janos said, "this is final?"

She nodded.

"I see," Janos said, "there is one more thing: Paris's horse . . . you've seen it?"

She nodded, and for the first time they both smiled a little and relaxed.

"Is remarkable," Janos breathed. Stepping back and addressing Paris as well, Janos said, "He works very much like you—from his heart."

Marina closed her eyes, "Please go."

He nodded to both of them and went out.

Paris looked to Marina impatiently, "What?"

"Please don't walk away from me any more," Marina entreated.

"I'm not, I'm right here," he said.

In a voice tinged with pain, she said, "I shouldn't have slapped you. I'm so sorry."

"It's okay, I forgot already," he lied, wanting to dispel her sadness more than anything.

"We have to move," she said, taking his face in her hands. They were strong and cool against his cheeks.

"But . . ."

"Please, Paris. If I thought there was the tiniest shred of hope . . . It's breaking my heart, too, but I need you to trust me now. I'm sorry we can't stay here, but I believe we can find someplace even better."

He took her hands from his face and held them. His fingers were already a little longer and thicker than hers. He wanted to do all he could for her.

"I'm with you, Mom," he said at last, "I'm not going to leave you like Dad."

She hugged him tightly.

"We have to go," she whispered.

"Okay," he whispered back, "okay."

CHAPTER FORTY EIGHT

Tommy was back from the Reservation up north. He had heard about the fire while he was away, but when he got back to Powderhorn, the first thing he wanted to see was Paris's horse. Like everyone, he was amazed by what Paris had accomplished. Since the garage was just about finished, and the last big cleanup was underway, Tommy turned his attention to the horse. He sanded the charred frame, gave it a saddle blanket, and adorned it with a leather halter and a single eagle feather. It looked majestic in a battle-tested war pony way.

Paris stood at the screen door and looked out on the now-familiar morning scene in his back yard, but not with the same enthusiasm of the past few days. Before today, his mother was going one way, and he and his neighbors were going another, but now he had promised to help her move on. She didn't walk away from him when he was a baby, or any number of hard times after that, and he couldn't walk away from her now.

The sight of Tommy took him pleasantly by surprise. He pushed open the door and called out to him. Tommy smiled and put his arm over the back of the horse, "Pretty elegant, no?"

Paris nodded and smiled, but he was feeling reluctant to join the crowd this morning. How was he going to tell his friends, who were so committed to helping them stay, that he and his mother really did have to move? He still didn't know as he approached Blossum, Pete and Janos. A hush fell over them, and Paris thought that Janos might already have told them about the bank's decision; in which case, they already understood that it was all over, and maybe Paris wouldn't have to say anything.

"Good! You are here, Paris," said Janos, "I'm talking about that header. Your mother says the bank won't give loan, but if we fix header, maybe they reconsider."

"What header?" Tommy asked, joining them.

"Listen, my mom's pretty tired," Paris said.

"Exactly," Janos said as though Paris were looking for agreement.

"I mean, she doesn't want to try any more," Paris added.

Janos balked, "But if we don't try, we never know. Is worth a try, no?"

Everyone was looking at Paris, and all he could feel was a churning in his gut.

"She says we really have to move, and . . ."

"Is somebody gonna tell me about this header?" Tommy asked.

Pete erupted, "Are we giving up here? 'Cause that is not okay!"

"Sounds that way," Blossum said simply.

Janos looked to Paris, "Tell us what you want us to do, and we'll do it."

Paris took a deep breath and chose his words carefully.

"If you think you can *really* fix it, and if you *really* think there might be a chance that the bank will give her the loan, then I say we go for it, and hope . . ."

"No time for hopin', Paris," Blossum said wisely, "We're goin' over the top."

Tommy offered to take over supervising the cleanup of the outside so that Janos, Pete, and Blossum could get to work inside.

"I feel like she's looking over my shoulder, like I'm trespassing," Pete said as he stared at the header.

"Stop being a ninny," Blossum said, "and start thinkin' about what to do here."

Janos winked at Paris, and they joined in their companions in looking up at the header. Eventually, Blossum stood apart, meditating, while the others wracked their brains for a good idea. Blossum fixed his gaze on the birdfeeder outside the dining room window, even though it was empty of seeds and there were no birds.

"Why can't we just put in a new one?" Paris finally asked in exasperation.

"We don't want to *replace* it if we can just *reinforce* it," Janos explained.

"So how do we do that?" Paris wanted to know.

Janos mumbled and moved to the other side of the header.

Pete barked, "Hey, Blossum, how 'bout some help?"

"I *am* helping," Blossum said, "It's talkin' to me."

Janos threw up his hands, "Please, be serious!"

"Be cool, man!" Blossum said unperturbed, "It needs steel," and with a wink to Pete he added, "Ten or twelve feet of it."

"And where we gonna find a piece of steel like that?" Pete demanded.

Blossum beamed slyly, "Saigon Garage."

"You devil!" Pete cried.

Janos turned to Paris, "I don't understand anything they just said."

"I'm talking about steel, and lots of it," Blossum repeated, heading for the door, "let's go!"

As they piled into Janos's truck, Pete explained, "The guy who owns the Saigon Garage is a good friend of ours. We're gonna try and barter for this thing."

"What *thing*?" Janos demanded, as he started the engine.

"You'll see," Blossum said, slamming his door shut.

"This better be real," Paris said as he settled in next to Pete in the cargo bay.

The Saigon Garage was real all right. The road leading up to it starts out as the driveway that leads to the city incinerator, snakes three-quarters of the way around the building, and veers off into a former factory site that has only one building left standing. There lies the garage. On the front wall is a faded map of Vietnam with a star presumably for the location of "former" Saigon. Above and below the map are the words SAIGON and GARAGE in big yellow letters lined in red. The rest of the property is a combination parking lot and machinery graveyard. At the far end is a retired boxcar. Nearby, lay several rusting dinosaurs that had once moved earth but are now sinking into it.

Blossum went into the office to conduct negotiations in private with Bao, the owner. When they came out of the office, both looked satisfied. Bao folded a piece of paper slid it into his shirt pocket, making sure to button down the flap. Whatever it was, the scrap of paper seemed to make him happy.

"We have a deal," Blossum announced to his friends, beaming.

Bao was a short, prosperous junk dealer, who had fled Saigon in the last days of the war, and found that his profession served him just as well in America as it had in Vietnam.

"Come with me," he said, leading them to a remote part of the yard, "and be amazed." They stopped before an altar-like something covered by a tarp that Bao removed reverently.

"1957 Cadillac," he said in a prayerful voice.

"Well, it's not *a* Cadillac," Blossum clarified for Paris and Janos, "it's pieces from the frame, to be exact—the steel that runs the length of one of the longest cars ever made."

"We can use this," Janos said approvingly, "I can get a jack from my construction site to lift the header, and slip this underneath. Is perfect solution!"

On the way home with their prize, Pete asked Blossum confidentially, "What'd you have to give him?"

"My hot sauce recipe."

As night fell, Paris watched Blossum work with the hunk of steel in his forge. This was deep, center-of-the-Earth magic like Paris had never seen before. Blossum's face was bathed in the brilliant glow, and Paris could feel the searing heat of the forge. Blossum pounded away at the superheated metal—straightening it, shaping it just so. He took on the elemental nature of his materials. His neck bulged, and his mouth contorted in a grimace. If he stopped to reach for a towel to wipe the sweat from his eyes, Paris offered him water, and he drank deeply from a small pail. Paris had never seen Blossum work so hard. The red-hot metal glowed in his eyes. The sparks coppered the air and his skin. His hammer fell with deadly force and precision. At last, wielding two sets of tongs, he lifted the hot metal and immersed it in a long trough of water and oil. This was located in a recess that Paris had never seen before because it was usually covered with an old canvas tent. A great cloud of steam rose up. The water hissed and bubbled violently, the tub itself rumbled with the force of the vibration.

CHAPTER FORTY NINE

"Is good!" Janos said with admiration, when he saw what Blossum had done with the length of steel.

"Good? Pizza is *good*; this is genius," Pete declared.

"Cut it out, Pete," Blossum said.

There was a moment of silence and some shuffling of feet as they turned to Janos.

"Okay," he began, "we will get this steel in position and get ready to push it into place. Then I inch up the header with jack."

Pete and Blossum took the ends and lifted the long steel beam over their heads. Pete stood on an upturned bucket to give him a little more height, and Paris helped in the middle, standing on a kitchen chair. Janos began pumping the jack handle. As the header creaked and the house groaned, the header moved upward only a fraction of an inch. They needed a little more clearance to slide in the reinforcing steel, but the house wouldn't yield any more. Blossum huffed and puffed and barely was able to slide his end partially into position, but it was not enough. Pete tried to do the same, but he was having a hard time balancing on the narrow top of a bucket. Janos joined Pete and tried to relieve him of some of the weight.

"I can't do it!" Pete gasped.

"What do you mean, *can't?*" Blossum grunted, still trying to force his end into place.

"I gotta go!" Pete grimaced, squeezing together his knees.

Three men and one boy, standing with their hands over their heads, their arms straining, and their faces contorted in pain: that was the way Marina found them. Her words sliced through the air, "What are you doing?"

"Mom, I didn't! I mean . . . I'm sorry, but . . ." Paris dithered.

"Marina," Janos began.

"Do *not* speak to me, any of you!" she commanded.

They wished they could be anywhere but here, ashamed and exposed before her.

"It's over! You have got to get OUT!" she cried.

"We CAN'T!" they yelled back.

Color drained from her face as she realized that they were truly stuck.

"Excuse me," Pete said, trying to be polite, "but I really have to go."

"He has to go to the bathroom," Blossum said through clenched teeth.

The men were beginning to wilt under the strain.

"Please go. None of this matters. It's not our house any more," she said.

"This is SO our house—they're trying to help us keep it. Why aren't you?" Paris blurted.

Seconds ticked by, and the header grew heavier.

"We can't hold this up much longer, Marina," Blossum said, "I brought my sledgehammer. It's there by the window. Get it, and hit the steel on my end to knock it in, under the header."

Paris held his breath as miraculously she didn't argue, but got ready to swing the sledgehammer.

"Just give us a count when you're ready," Blossum said, "I'm closing my eyes now. It's up to you."

Marina took a deep breath, "Ready on three. One, two, three!"

WHAM! She slammed the steel bar into place over Blossum's head.

"Over here now," Janos urged quickly, pointing to the spot over Pete's head.

WHAM!

"Great, Mom!" Paris shouted.

"What next?" Marina asked, looking to Blossum.

"Just tap each end in so the steel is flush with the header," Blossum said, and the men moved out of her way.

"Nice! Pete blurted, "Now, where's the john?"

"Upstairs," Paris said.

They laughed as Pete ran awkwardly for the stairs. Marina turned to Blossum, "What *is* that thing holding up my house, and where did you get it?"

"A '57 Cadillac . . ." Blossum grinned.

"Do I owe you money?" Marina asked.

"No, Mom. Blossum paid for it with hot sauce," Paris laughed.

"It's okay, Marina," Blossum said in response to Marina's puzzled look, "there was no money involved."

Upstairs, the toilet flushed, and shortly thereafter Pete reappeared.

"That's it," he said, "We've got to move on. You comin', Blossum?"

With an enormous smile on his face, Blossum turned and nodded to each of them on his way out, "See you later, Paris, Marina, Janos."

CHAPTER FIFTY

"Hello, Mr. Holmgren. It's Marina Thibideaux. I'm calling because I'd like to renew my loan application."

Paris gave his mother a double thumbs-up.

"We've rebuilt the garage, fixed the header, and we're working on the soffits and gutters."

Paris stood looking out the back door at the garage while listening to the rest of her conversation. It was part old school bus and several rows of recycled paving bricks. Aluminum siding in an array of pastels left over from numerous jobs in the neighborhood was featured, as well as farmhouse windows and a Victorian screen door that hadn't seen the light of day in eighty years. The roof was a patchwork of leftover shingles from at least ten roofing jobs in the neighborhood, and someone had made window boxes out of dresser drawers painted red.

"Well," Marina said after listening for a while, "all I'm asking for is an inspection. You said yourself that I've done a lot of good work on this house."

Marina rapped her fingers impatiently on the counter. Paris didn't have to look to know that she was growing impatient.

"Yes, I know Mr. Ermler's deadline is Saturday afternoon," she said at last, "Can you come on Saturday morning?"

Paris turned and saw in her eyes that they were back in the game.

"Thanks so much!" Marina said warmly, reaching out to give Paris's arm a squeeze, "Yes, I understand that you can't promise anything. We'd just like a chance to show you what we've done." She hung up.

"You did it!" Paris said as she danced around the kitchen.

"We'll see," she said, breathlessly falling into a chair, "we've got a lot of work to do."

"Thanks, Mom," Paris said.

"It might not work," she said, "you know that, right?"

"I do," he said.

"I'm not sure he's going to appreciate the garage the way we do because if it had wheels, it might win a prize in the Parade," Marina added lightheartedly.

With the parade only days away, everyone else along the alley was trying frantically to finish their own projects, but Janos came and worked on the Thibideaux house just about every possible hour that he wasn't working at his regular job. He and Marina worked well together, as long as they kept conversation to a minimum. Paris noticed that anything much beyond "Pass me the hammer," tended to fizzle. And when Janos started patching the gouges she had made in the drywall, Paris could tell that Marina was embarrassed and didn't want him cleaning up her mess.

"I can do that," she said, but Janos simply moved over and said, "Sure, we get done twice as fast." He made room for her to join him, and she did.

"Stay for dinner," she said when they were finished, "you've put in long day."

"No, no," Janos said quickly. It was his habit.

"We'd really like you to stay," Paris said hopefully. It wasn't the first time he had been invited, and he always refused. But by now

Paris was so grateful for Janos's help that he was willing to accept that some questions about the man might never be answered, and this was probably one of them.

Then one evening, after dark, Paris was on his way to return some tools to Janos. It was a nice summer night, and he approached the stairs leading to Janos's balcony with the canvas carry-bag of tools in hand. Janos and Blossum were on the porch talking and laughing, and it seemed like a good sign to Paris that Janos had made a friend and settled in. He was about to announce his presence when he heard his mother's name and froze.

"Marina sure is an amazing woman," Blossum said.

"Sure, yes," Janos said.

"You're the first guy she's ever worked with on that house," Blossum continued. *That's not exactly true,* Paris thought, *but Janos is the only one to last more than an hour.*

"If you drink my whiskey and sit on my porch, you should change subject," Janos said flatly.

"Come on," Blossum insisted, "what do you think about her?"

"Marina works hard," Janos said cautiously, "and she does good work."

"That's it?" Blossum's voice rose in consternation.

"That's it," Janos said.

"Well, I don't know your story—and I probably never will—but I know this: you are one broken-hearted bastard."

"Blossum, my friend, you *don't* know my story," said Janos lifting his glass.

"Nor you, mine, my friend," Blossum replied mysteriously, meeting Janos's glass with his own and producing a satisfying clink.

Paris backed away silently from the stairs. The tools could wait until morning. He understood now that Janos wanted no part of neighborhood gossip. It was like in school if a boy is friends with a girl, or races her on the playground, everyone starts saying he's in love. He could understand Janos wanting to avoid that kind of nonsense, but if Blossum was already teasing Janos about Marina, Paris thought, the neighborhood gossip machine was already running.

There was another reason, though—known only to Janos—why he didn't linger with Paris and Marina after the day's work was done. Even as he sat there with Blossum, more involved with people than he had been in years, Janos had a letter on his kitchen table offering him a new job in Chicago.

CHAPTER FIFTY ONE

Parade Day finally dawned. From all parts of the Powderhorn Neighborhood, giant puppets and stilt walkers would soon converge on the staging area; and, by early afternoon the parade would begin to uncoil like a great snake on its way to the park. Across the alley, Mrs. Vang had draped the flowing silks of a great water dragon over bushes and lawn furniture. All it needed was the dancing legs of children to bring it to life. At the other end of the alley, Randi and the kids had loaded their pirate ship on to the back of a flatbed truck.

There had been a number of minor explosions at Pete and Blossum's place, and Pete had lost his eyebrows to whatever-it-was that he and Blossum were making for the parade. Nevertheless, undeterred, Blossum got his barrel smoker going early in the day, and the aromas reminded all of the alley neighbors of the feast that would follow the parade.

Helen Torvilson was sitting at her kitchen table, finishing a cup of coffee that was no longer hot, when she saw a boy lurking outside her back gate. For a moment she was thrown back in time to when boys would come and go all day, looking for Danny and Tommy, and sometimes stay to supper. Harold McNaughton. She wished she had been able to help that boy more, but she was so busy with her own family back then. Now, Billy was out in that same alley, up to God-knew-what. He used to prowl the alley like he owned it, but something had happened to him. These days he skulked around like a hungry dog at a picnic. She was halfway down the walk, calling out to him, before she knew it.

"Billy, come here, I want to talk to you!"

Startled, Billy didn't even think to run away.

"I have a proposition for you," she said pleasantly.

"No kidding," Billy said coolly, but his heart was racing. Most people didn't speak to him in conversational tones.

"You broke this gate, and I expect you to fix it," she said, coming into the driveway and stopping right in front of him.

"No way," Billy scoffed, but her eyes kept him riveted to the spot.

"I'm not asking, young man," Helen said, "you owe me."

"Pay me and I'll do it," Billy said to see if he could make her mad.

"I'll make you supper," she countered.

"I eat at home," Billy insisted.

"Your father cooks for you, does he?" Helen asked, skeptically.

Billy had to laugh at that.

"What if I don't like your cookin'?" he smirked.

"All boys like my cooking," Helen declared, "you come tomorrow. I'll expect you."

Billy had never had such an offer, and his confusion showed on his face.

"You come tomorrow," Helen said, sensing a struggle going on in the boy, "and I'll throw in a pie."

"I hate pie," he lied.

"What then?" Helen asked.

"I can't do it, I don't have any tools," he said.

"I've got all the tools you need," Helen assured him. She could almost see the gears turning as he weighed his options.

"Pie's okay then," he said at last.

"Then, pie it is," she said.

CHAPTER FIFTY TWO

For Paris and his mother the parade might as well have been on the moon. They were preparing to win or lose their home, and they prepared like warriors before the last battle of the war. Like a wandering knight, Janos was with them, helping to get everything as close to finished as possible before the man from the bank arrived. As the hour approached, Paris was posted as a lookout near the front of the house.

"That's it," Marina said, as she and Janos came down from their ladders at the same time. She stared at his last repair job.

"How did you get that last piece to fit?" she asked.

"Which?" Janos asked distractedly, rooting for something in his toolbox.

She pointed, "That one . . . what's holding it up there?"

"I use Play-Doh," Janos said with a shrug, "Looks okay now. Fix it better, later."

Neither could tell what the other was thinking, until laughter overtook them both. Just then, Paris came running around the corner of the house.

"Mom, Mr. Holmgren's here!"

"Go!" Janos said, taking down the ladder, "Take him inside. Paris and I finish out here."

"Go!" Paris chimed in, shooing her away.

"Tool belt!" Janos said, pointing at her hips.

"Oh!" Marina laughed nervously as she fumbled with the buckle. Paris yanked it from her and slung it over his shoulder.

"How do I look?" she asked, smoothing her hair with her hands.

"Great!" Paris and Janos exclaimed. Then, they hurried about cleaning up the evidence of their last-minute labors.

"Thanks for coming, Mr. Holmgren," Marina said warmly, extending her hand.

Holmgren was clearly frazzled, "I forgot all about the parade and the detours."

"How about some iced tea while I show you around?" she offered.

"No thanks, Mrs. Thibideaux, I really have very little time. Just show me the header, and then we can move on to the exterior elements."

"Fine," she said agreeably, although she was a little worried about his curt manner. He went straight to the header.

"We left it partially exposed so you could see it," Marina said confidently, trying not to show any fear.

"What am I looking at exactly?" Holmgren asked, "Steel?"

Marina did not want to say the word *Cadillac* so she simply said, "Yes."

Holmgren inspected it closely, stepping back to look at it from various angles. Unable to suppress his curiosity, Paris appeared at the window. Marina shooed him away, and he disappeared unnoticed by the bank man. After a lot of writing on his clipboard, Mr. Holmgren still looked puzzled.

"Is something wrong?" Marina asked, eyeing the window and hoping Paris would have the good sense to remain invisible.

Holmgren shook his head, "I've never seen it done quite like this," he said, "it's *odd*. I'd like to move on to the gutters now."

"You don't want to look over the kitchen?" Marina asked, "Or anything else inside? We've done so much."

She was stalling to give Paris and Janos time to bring some order to the back yard, but Holmgren seemed to be in a hurry.

He sighed impatiently and said, "I know you do good work, but the bank is most interested in the integrity of structural elements, the gutters and soffits, and the garage. That's really all I need to see."

"Oh . . ." Marina said, fading.

"Mrs. Thibideaux," Holmgren paused, unfolding a hanky from his pocket and wiping his brow, "this is about meeting the bank's standards for borrowing money, plain and simple."

He wished he could tell her not to worry, but he already knew which way the bank was leaning. He had worked there long enough to know that if he wanted to get ahead at the bank, he had to show that he wasn't a pushover for a single mother in distress.

"Let's start with the gutters out front and work our way around back," Marina suggested. Mr. Holmgren stared up at the soffits, took notes, shook the downspouts until they rattled, and wrote some more. Meanwhile, in the back yard, Paris and Janos stashed the tools on the back porch, stored the ladders inside the garage, and tidied up the last pile of wrecked gutters.

"Mrs. Thibideaux, hello!" Janos said, as he and Paris pretended to be surprised, "We will remove damaged gutters on Monday, if that's all right with you."

"Are you the contractor?" Mr. Holmgren asked, brightening.

"Yes," Janos said quickly, "I live next door."

"Oh, a friend," Holmgren concluded.

Janos looked at Paris and Marina, "Yes. I am contractor *and* friend."

"Did you work on the garage?" Holmgren asked.

"Yes," Janos said, "I helped to design and build it."

As the weary banker approached the garage, Paris, Marina, and Janos looked warily at one another. Taking off his glasses, Holmgren asked, "Is that part of a school bus?"

"Yes, it is," answered Pete, striding in from the alley, bare-chested, wearing plaid shorts, and black high-top sneakers. Brass tubes snaked around his body and over his shoulders and flared out into a large tuba-shaped opening. Wisps of smoke drifted from their gullets.

"I'm Pete Chavez, neighbor across the alley, and you are . . ."

"Gordon Holmgren, Tri-County Trust," Holmgren replied.

Pete's hair was slicked back dramatically, and he wore a perpetually surprised look since he had singed off his eyebrows.

"Do you mind if I call you Gordon?" he asked, pumping the man's hand vigorously, "and you can call me Pete."

"No, I don't mind," Mr. Holmgren murmured.

"This building is a work of art, Gordon," Pete enthused, drawing the reluctant bank man out into the alley, "The neighborhood is darn proud of it. It's an attractive-if-whimsical design that is well-built *and* functional."

Marina and Janos were dumbfounded, but Paris grinned as if to say *relax, we are watching a master at work.*

And Pete did not disappoint.

"Now, I can see by your bow tie that you're a man who doesn't like surprises," he practically crooned, "and this building looks like it's full of 'em, right? But if you give it a close examination, you'll see that it is well constructed."

He led Mr. Holmgren to a window and urged him to peer inside.

"There are solid welds in the interior framing that would make the Gods weep!" he rhapsodized.

"Yes, but what about structural integrity?" Holmgren muttered.

"Gordon," Pete crooned like a car salesman, "This garage has craftsmanship fit for *Architectural Digest*. Look at the perfect hydraulics of this school bus door! Go ahead, try it."

"That's not necessary, Mr. Chavez," Holmgren said, backing away from Pete, only to bump into a big man in beaded and feathered Ojibwe ceremonial garb. He approached supernatural proportions in the eyes of Mr. Holmgren, who now yanked off his clip-on tie, and stuffed it into a pocket. He unbuttoned the top button of his shirt and took a deep breath. Paris and Janos understood that the neighbors had orchestrated a kind of tag-team wrestling match approach to dealing with Mr. Holmgren, but Marina knew nothing of tag-teams or wrestling, and she began to feel as though her world was spinning out of control. Right now, it was in Tommy's hands.

"Thomas Browneagle," Tommy introduced himself, and then gestured toward the garage, "impressive, ennit?"

"Gordon Holmgren," the bank man said as they shook hands. Tommy grasped Holmgren's elbow and gently led him a few steps away for a confidential chat.

"I think it's best, Gordon, to view this as much more than a garage," Tommy said persuasively, "It's a formal expression of our community, and *your* bank, the Tri-County *Trust*, needs to live up to its name here with Mrs. Thibideaux."

"I'm not sure what you mean," Gordon remarked earnestly, as he sucked in his gut and tried to stand taller.

Tommy sighed, "Let's be clear, Gordon, shall we? You know this house, as well as I do. Before Marina and her boy moved in, it was a drug house and an eyesore. Felix Ermler has been a poor steward of this property, and everyone else on the block has paid the price for it."

Paris couldn't make out what Tommy was saying, but he could tell that what had seemed a few moments earlier like typical Powderhorn humor, had turned more serious. Almost as if Tommy had conjured them, a crowd in parade costume began to gather around the two men. Mr. Holmgren stopped speaking and scanned the faces nervously. He soon recognized many of them as bank customers, however, and relaxed.

Tommy spoke up now so everyone nearby could hear.

"We want Marina to stay in Powderhorn; and, you should want her to stay, too. She works hard. She invests in her home, and she'll be a good customer for years to come. So, it's time to decide—Marina and Paris Thibideaux, or the parasite Ermler? We're watching," he concluded, pointing to his own eye significantly.

"Thank you, Mr. Browneagle," Holmgren said. He knew what the bank and Felix Ermler expected him to do, but he couldn't justify doing it. What they wanted was not right, but if he did it, he would be rewarded. If he didn't, well that would be his problem.

He turned from the crowd in the alley and walked back through the Thibideaux yard like he had the weight of the world on his shoulders. He walked past Marina and Paris without looking up, and continued to his car parked in front of the house. Just as he clicked his pen and began writing on his clipboard, a child's voice called out.

"Mr. Holmgren, wait!" Paris cried impulsively, running to him. Marina was right behind him.

Holmgren looked up startled, "Yes?"

"Mr. Holmgren, you've got to talk to my mother," Paris pleaded, "I mean, you can't just . . ."

Suddenly, Holmgren realized that he'd made up his mind, but no one knew what he had decided.

Paris snatched the pen from Holmgren's hand, "It's not fair!"

Holmgren looked at Paris and shook his head, "You're right, son. I'm sorry, Mrs. Thibideaux, I shouldn't have just started scribbling."

"I just want to know if there's anything more I can do?" Marina said with as much dignity as she could muster.

"You've done enough, Mrs. Thibideaux," he replied, holding his hand out for the pen, which Paris reluctantly returned.

"Thank you," he said flipping pages on his clipboard, scribbling his initials in various places, and finally signing on one of the lines.

"We're not going by the book here," he said, handing over the papers to Marina.

"Oh," Marina said weakly, absently passing them to Paris who grabbed them eagerly and began to read.

"Your loan is approved," Mr. Holmgren said kindly, "We'll close next week. In the meantime, this paperwork should satisfy Mr. Ermler."

Marina grabbed the papers from Paris's hands and stared at them, "Does it really say that?"

"It really does," Mr. Holmgren assured her.

"Thank you, Mr. Holmgren," she said, and she hugged him.

"You're welcome," Holmgren replied with an awkward smile. He shook hands with Paris, and said, "The neighborhood is lucky to have both of you."

They pretended to be calm until he turned the corner. Then they broke into a run toward the back yard. Marina's hair flew wildly behind her, as she waved the loan papers over her head like a trophy. Janos planted his feet firmly, but even he couldn't resist the momentum of Marina and Paris. They clasped his hands and drew him into their jumping, hopping, dance of happiness, and before he knew it, he had his arms around them.

CHAPTER FIFTY THREE

Paris felt like he was in a dream, free falling without fear. He had felt like this once before—when he was at the State Fair cresting the highest peak of the giant roller coaster. It was the unseen force of happiness lifting him and everyone around him. Neighbors poured in from the alley, drawn to the crazy joy that had erupted in the Thibideaux yard. Marina was inundated with hugs and congratulations when she told about getting the loan.

"You won, Sweetie!" Randi crowed enthusiastically, "Does Ermler know?"

Marina held up the loan papers confidently, "He will soon!"

Paris could see in the eyes of his neighbors, admiration for his mother and, he was sure, gratitude for ridding the block of Felix Ermler. Paris believed that this was the best day of his life.

People began to leave to get back to their Parade activities, and soon it was just Paris, Janos, and Marina standing alone in the yard again.

"So what now?" Janos asked.

Before Marina could speak, the answer came in the form of a car horn blasting away insistently in front of the house.

"Oh, my God," Marina exclaimed, "Ermler!"

She clutched the precious loan papers to her heart and ran toward the front of the house. Paris ran after her, but Janos stayed behind, not sure what to do. Felix Ermler sat in his sealed-up air-conditioned car, leaning on his horn. Paris noticed that some of the neighbors, who should be on their way to the Parade by now, had stopped to stare. More troubling, however, was the presence of Billy McNaughton sitting on the roof across the street, looking right back at him. His stomach cramped as if grasped by a cold fist.

Felix took his hand off the horn and rolled down his window as Marina approached, "Why are you still here? Do I have to call the police to get you out?"

"We're here because the bank approved my loan," she said proudly.

"I doubt that," Felix sneered.

"I can pay you everything that I owe," Marina said firmly, "Mr. Holmgren said you should be satisfied with these."

He snatched them from her hand and rolled up the window. Paris could see that Ermler was growing more agitated, and his mother was getting more nervous. Finally, the window slid down, and he tossed the papers from the car.

"Even if this loan is any good, which I *question*, it doesn't cover everything you owe."

"What?" Marina gasped, as Paris gathered up the papers.

"Five hundred and seventy-six dollars and ninety-eight cents," Felix said, "to cover my service fees, penalties, and repairs."

"What are you talking about?" Marina demanded.

"Read the contract," Felix declared, "You signed it."

He tapped the face of his wristwatch, "Tick-Tock. You're supposed to vacate by noon. You have seventeen minutes to get out."

"This is bullshit!" Paris declared, and Ermler's window flew back up.

Marina stood stiff and silent. Either she hadn't heard him, or she agreed with him—he wasn't sure which. The small crowd of neighbors that had been gathering began to grumble in the background and to move in closer to surround Ermler's car. They were making him nervous. He revved the engine a few times, menacingly. Suddenly, a rock came hurtling out of nowhere and shattered Ermler's windshield. Felix ducked and covered his head as though he'd been shot.

Like everyone close to the car, Paris jumped back in alarm and pulled his mother along with him. The crowd was churning with fear and anger, a dangerous mix. No one recognized the signs better than Janos. He came forward and slapped a hard, flat hand on the roof of the car. At the same time, he searched the faces in the crowd and scanned the rooftops and trees, but the stone thrower had escaped or blended in by now. Paris had seen Janos this angry only once before, when Billy stole his camera.

"Knock it off!" Janos roared to the crowd, which hushed immediately, "No more of that, you hear?"

From inside his car, Ermler looked up at Janos gratefully. He lowered the window and said, "They tried to kill me!"

Leaning down close to Ermler's face, Janos said, "No one's trying to kill you, Mr. Wormle. Someone threw a rock. You're fine."

Ermler sat up and gripped the wheel with both hands. He looked straight ahead, apparently refusing to communicate, but Janos was unmoved.

"So, how much does Mrs. Thibideaux owe you?"

Ermler seethed, "Who the hell are you?"

"How much money does Mrs. Thibideaux still owe you?" Janos asked again.

"This is between me and her," Felix bristled, "And the name's *ERMler*!"

Janos pounded his fist on the roof. Felix flinched and began to sweat.

"How much?" Janos demanded.

There were three things Felix Ermler always avoided as part of his standard business practice: witnesses, challenges, and men who looked like they could hurt him.

"Call it an even five hundred," Felix snarled, "but if she doesn't have it by Noon, the house is mine. She signed a contract."

The window went up.

"People!" Janos addressed the crowd, "We've got ten minutes to collect five hundred dollars for the Thibideaux family. I've got forty-three, no forty-eight dollars!" he shouted, holding up the bills for all to see.

"I've got money in my cookie jar!" Randi shouted.

"Us, too!" Blossum said.

"I got twenty-seven right here!" Pete added, handing the cash to Janos.

"Can we borrow this?" Janos asked, sweeping a baseball cap from a boy's head.

"Sure, take it," Billy said, "and *here*," he added, as he stuffed a handful of bills into the cap.

"This is a lot of money," Janos said to Billy, "are you sure?"

Billy looked straight at Ermler and said, "Yeah, I'm sure."

Janos turned to Paris, "Is okay?"

Paris knew he should thank Billy, but the words just wouldn't come out of his mouth. He nodded, and Billy nodded in reply.

"Is good," Janos said, as he took a seat on the hood of Ermler's car.

Paris and Marina watched their friends rush home and come back with their money. Billy's cap filled steadily, although Billy himself had slipped away. Janos dumped the cash on the hood of Ermler's car and began to count it. Coins clattered and scraped across the mirror finish. The car window rolled down.

"Time's up!" Felix crowed.

Janos scooped the money back into the cap. Marina clasped Paris's hand and closed her eyes when Janos offered the money to Ermler.

"We're fifty-three dollars short," he said, "We get it for you . . ."

"No deal!" Felix said to Marina, "I give you and the boy an hour to clear out!"

Then, WHRRRT! Up went the window. All eyes turned suddenly, toward a shrill voice piercing the air. Mrs. Vang appeared, swinging a heavy cloth bag from side to side, parting the crowd in a path that led straight to Ermler.

"Oh, for god's sake, it's Mulan," Felix huffed.

Mrs. Vang counted off fifty-three dollars from a wad of bills, and waved it in front of the window. Ermler scowled and opened it part way. She thrust the money at him, and he took it.

"Receipt!" she demanded.

"For five hundred dollars!" Janos added, dumping the rest of the money in Ermler's lap. Ermler re-counted the money and tore a receipt from his book. Mrs. Vang held it up for all to see, then handed it to Marina.

"I don't know what to say," Marina whispered.

Mrs. Vang put a finger to her lips and shook her head.

The crowd opened up for Ermler to drive away. Marina began thanking her neighbors and promising to pay them back, but people seemed more interested in getting to the Parade.

"I don't understand," she said to Helen Torvilson.

Helen said, "You don't pay back a blessing, Marina. You just pass it on."

Marina turned to Paris, but he was no longer at her side. He was running toward Janos.

"I have a great idea!" he announced with enthusiasm.

"Of course, you do," Janos laughed.

"What if you use half of our garage for your workshop, and I use the other half for mine. Wouldn't that be great?"

"Wow! Is very generous offer, but," he hesitated, looking from one expectant face to the other, "I am leaving, to go to work in Chicago."

Paris looked confused.

"I have another job," Janos went on, "Is what I do."

"Why?" Paris demanded, "Why can't you stay here?"

Janos tried to say what he had planned to say, but with Marina and Paris looking at him so intently, it didn't seem right.

"When?" Paris asked coldly.

"Soon," Janos said, "Couple weeks."

Paris could not speak, so he ran.

CHAPTER FIFTY FOUR

J anos went looking for Paris. He ran past the horse the boy had created and he went into the garage. It was quiet, except for the distant and muffled sounds of the Parade. Despite his earliest doubts, he marveled at the neighborhood's achievement. They had built a serviceable garage in a very short time. Inside, they'd roughed out plenty of shelves and an extra long workbench for Paris. They had replaced the cupola with a high window to let in plenty of light. On a platform under the window, he found Paris.

"How's the view?" he asked.

Paris didn't answer, but the inclination of his head indicated to Janos that he was listening.

"The Parade's started," Janos said.

"I know," said Paris without turning.

"I thought we could watch it together," Janos said, "We're just about the only ones not in it."

Paris continued staring out the window, swallowing hard to keep his tears down.

"I can watch it from here," he said, which they both knew was not true.

"You don't make sense," Janos said.

"YOU don't!" Paris shot back.

Janos scratched his head. Whatever persuasive skill he had once had with children eluded him now. He checked his watch, and inquired, "Can you tell me if there is a truck coming up the alley?"

"Seriously?" Paris asked, turning to give him a withering look.

"I'm expecting something to be delivered," Janos said lamely.

Indeed, a truck with a trailer attached was struggling to make the sharp turn from the street into the alley.

"Yeah, it's out there," Paris said, "the guy can't drive worth spit, though."

"It's a *lady*, and I won't tell her you said so," Janos said. He went out and greeted the driver and he helped her open the trailer. Paris knew what kind of trailer it was, but he hardly dared to think what was inside. The driver was a woman he had seen working at the park. She unloaded the ramp and climbed into the trailer. Paris's eyes opened wide as a chestnut-colored horse backed down the ramp right in Max's driveway. Her coat glistened in the sunlight and her mane and tail had been braided with ribbons. She was dressed up for the Parade. As he watched Janos take the lead line from the driver, Paris felt all the anger drain from his body. He reminded himself that Janos was still an impossible man—stern and distant one day and extremely generous the next. And now he was going to leave Powderhorn!

He burst out of the garage, barely able to speak.

"Janos!" he barked, indicating the horse, "What the heck?"

The horse nickered, and Janos turned to her and said, "I told you he would come down for you."

The horse lowered her head familiarly for a scratch under the forelock. Then, Paris buried his face in her neck.

"Come...I give you a hand up," Janos said after a few moments had passed, but Paris fell against him and put his arms around his waist. The hug only lasted a few seconds. Then, Janos made a step with his hands and boosted Paris into the saddle. He tightened the girth and adjusted the stirrups. Paris was filled with love for the horse and the excitement of being able to ride her in the Parade, but there was no separating this miracle from Janos, and Janos was going away. Tears threatened to spill on to his cheeks, but he managed to blink them back.

"This horse has been in many parades, so she is easy to lead," he said, "Are you ready?"

Paris nodded, and Janos led the way down the alley.

"Thank you," Paris said hoarsely, but he couldn't be heard above the drums and music of the Parade that hit them like a wall of sound when they reached the end of the alley. Janos looked for an opening in the line of the Parade while Paris scanned the crowd for his mother. Suddenly two pillars of fire shot into the air with a thunderous roar. It was Pete and Blossum and their homemade flambeaus.

"Son of a gun!" Pete exclaimed when he saw Paris on the back of the beautiful horse, "What a beauty!"

Blossum saluted with three short blasts of fire. At the next intersection, the Parade halted and opened up a "playing area" for the guys. Accompanied by a Reggae band, they blasted howling balls of fire into the air in time with the music. As in previous years, the crowd responded to the spectacle with raucous cheers and applause, which only encouraged Pete to attempt ever more complex acrobatic feats while spouting fire from his flambeau.

Paris and Janos moved through the crowd, looking for an opportunity to join the procession. It came by way of a giant puppet known as Mother Earth. Animated by three puppeteers, she bowed graciously and made way for them. They found themselves in a sea of pale blue silk ribbons and gauze sheets suspended between figures dressed in puffy white costumes representing clouds. The display was known as "The Heavens," and it always followed Mother Earth in the parade. Among the clouds and blue sky, musicians played flutes and triangles, and the tiny bells on their ankles added a rhythm so light that it suggested wind or flowing water. For Paris, the effect was otherworldly, like riding among the clouds, and the horse moved easily so that she seemed to be dancing.

Suddenly, Marina appeared. The heavenly blue sheets and ribbons parted for her. She had a circlet of delicate white flowers nestled in her hair, and from her shoulders bright silks flowed—white and pink and pale, pale green. Janos saw her, too, and reached out a hand to pull her alongside.

"Mom!" Paris cried, "Look!"

"Beautiful!" Marina shouted, turning to Janos, "Thank you!"

He smiled, not sure what she had said; but he held on to her hand as they were surrounded and passed by the Mayan dancers in their feathered headdresses. Then came the Morris dancers with bells on their arms and legs, a marching jazz band, floats, puppets, acrobats, and singers. Sometimes their songs and rhythms blended; sometimes they competed.

The sound of a drum group approaching made Paris turn just in time to see Tommy in the lead carrying the flag of the American Indian Movement. And walking with the drummers and their big drums was Helen wearing Danny's American flag over her shoulders. Most surprising of all, was the companion marching next to her: Billy McNaughton. He turned to meet Paris's eyes, and it was a little easier this time for both of them. Perhaps they could never be friends, but they were no longer enemies.

As the Parade came to its end at Powderhorn Park, a human tide of thousands swelled at the entrance. Janos shortened his lead on the horse and held it tight. With his other hand he pulled Marina closer to keep her from being swept away. She smiled up at Paris, and he thought she had never looked so happy. As they moved with the crowd into the Park, and the expanse of the lake spread out before them, Paris felt as though the World of Lost Things had opened up and out walked this Parade of Life.

"Hey, Paris! Paris!" someone called out. It was a familiar voice, he was sure of it. His eyes darted among the sea of faces, and the horse whinnied and shook her head like she'd heard it too.

"Over hear, Buddy," he heard, and a cough, "Over here." It was Dan's voice, but that was impossible. Suddenly, a blinding camera

209

flash went off in his face. It caught Marina and Janos too. Before the spots cleared from his eyes, Paris felt the unmistakable presence of a friend. It poured in like water and filled him with joy.

EPILOGUE

No one knows who took it. It was in a random collection of photographs of the Parade that year. It hangs in a frame on the wall now. It's not Christmas or Thanksgiving or a wedding, although those events would follow from it. It's just a photograph of three happy people in the midst of a neighborhood celebration in the mixed-up, crazy, colorful heart of the City—Paris, Marina, and Janos. It's the moment they moved beyond all that they had lost or suffered, and allowed themselves to be Found.